WI 9/22
LOCAL AUTHOR

WITNEY LIBRARY
Welch Way
Witney
Oxon OX28 6JH

Tel: 01993 703650

To renew this book, phone 0845 1202811 or visit
our website at www.libcat.oxfordshire.gov.uk
(for both options you will need your library PIN
number available from your library),
or contact any Oxfordshire library

OXFORDSHIRE
COUNTY COUNCIL

L017-64 (01/13)

Also by Peter Massam

Learning Experience Trilogy
Nipper (2022)
ISBN–13: 978-1-9822-8609-5

First Cuz Collection of Poems
Sketch Poems (2019; Audible 2020)
ISBN–13: 978–1701299238

Second Cuz Collection of Poems
Reflections in a Country Garden (2021)
ISBN–13: 979–8723096103

Customer Experience
Managing Service Level Quality across Wireless and Fixed Networks (2002)
ISBN–13: 978–0470848487

Learning Experience Series

This volume forms part of a trilogy:

> *Nipper*
> *Moose Conquering Fear*
> *Know Your Mind*

They track a lifetime journey of learning experiences from childhood encounters through coming of age to conquering fear, which culminate in a new appreciation of the power of the mind in the realms of communication, pain relief and self-help healing and preservation.

MOOSE
CONQUERING FEAR

PETER MASSAM

BALBOA.PRESS
A DIVISION OF HAY HOUSE

Copyright © 2022 Peter Massam.

All rights reserved. No part of this book may be used or reproduced by any means, graphic, electronic, or mechanical, including photocopying, recording, taping or by any information storage retrieval system without the written permission of the author except in the case of brief quotations embodied in critical articles and reviews.

Balboa Press books may be ordered through booksellers or by contacting:

Balboa Press
A Division of Hay House
1663 Liberty Drive
Bloomington, IN 47403
www.balboapress.co.uk
UK TFN: 0800 0148647 (Toll Free inside the UK)
UK Local: (02) 0369 56325 (+44 20 3695 6325 from outside the UK)

Because of the dynamic nature of the Internet, any web addresses or links contained in this book may have changed since publication and may no longer be valid. The views expressed in this work are solely those of the author and do not necessarily reflect the views of the publisher, and the publisher hereby disclaims any responsibility for them.

The author of this book does not dispense medical advice or prescribe the use of any technique as a form of treatment for physical, emotional, or medical problems without the advice of a physician, either directly or indirectly. The intent of the author is only to offer information of a general nature to help you in your quest for emotional and spiritual well-being. In the event you use any of the information in this book for yourself, which is your constitutional right, the author and the publisher assume no responsibility for your actions.

Any people depicted in stock imagery provided by Getty Images are models, and such images are being used for illustrative purposes only. Certain stock imagery © Getty Images.

Print information available on the last page.

ISBN: 978-1-9822-8628-6 (sc)
ISBN: 978-1-9822-8630-9 (hc)
ISBN: 978-1-9822-8629-3 (e)

Balboa Press rev. date: 08/17/2022

Dedication

For Harold, for Sue and Pete for always being there and for my Family

Contents

Dedication v
Preface ix
Introduction xi

Moose Conquering Fear

A la Recherche du Soulagement 1
Too Many Teeth 2
A Water Baby 4
Going the Extra 250 Miles 6
The Three Stooges 9
Gills Perch 11
Running and Rowing 14
The Bollard Tree 16
The Group of Six 22
Priory Pals 26
Second Year Immersion 29
Planning Ahead 33
Off to France 37
Another Day 42
Life in Burgundy 45
Life on the Factory Floor 49
A birthday like no other 53
Three Months In 56
Heading Out and About 60
Butterfly Wide Open 63
Singing a New Song 68
Love the One you're with 74
Doing Just Enough 76
Surrey Days 79
First Encounter of the Close Kind 85
Change of Scenery 90
Return to Abnormality 95
Out of the Blue 99
New Outlook 103
Parting 106
New Beginnings 109

About the Author 111

Preface

This series was conceived on the back of a business career that developed a customer strategy based on experience as a key factor. This was at a time when the concept of *customer experience* was thought to be inconsequential in a business setting.

After only a few years evangelising the concept, it was pleasing to see it feature subsequently as a permanent agenda item at board level. However, it became increasingly apparent that industries – the telecommunications sector and their partners in my case – were struggling to come to terms with the softer elements affecting customer acquisition, engagement and retention. The old operational adage *'if you can't measure it, you can't manage it'* was superfluous in the feeling and trust domains.

Understanding the customer mindset and therefore the ways in which the mind worked is entirely new territory for them: an area where a psychologist would, quite reasonably, feel right at home.

Having no such psychology degree but with a strong interest in the mind's influence over our everyday life, I fell back on my personal experience to recount former experiences and the thoughts which pervaded those situations.

Initially these were focussed on emotions naturally and the interactions between people. The link between the physical world, the senses and the mind that assimilates, filters and stores information presented to it drew a parallel with aspects of my previous work in analysing complex data sets.

With the onset of the pandemic in 2019-20, coupled with previously known disturbing occurrences of suicide in young students, I felt it may help to bring some focus onto the well-being of that very sensitive attribute that we all possess, but possibly underestimate its capabilities: the mind.

Introduction

This part moves on from the growing pains and obstacles to forming first relationships to record moments of fear and exhilaration experienced by the same person, George, during his student days, during a year working abroad as part of the course and beyond.

It is as easy to fall into a working life as it is into a new relationship, from which springs eternal the hope that both will last. Choosing 'safe' over 'fear of losing' can result in an increasing sense of uneasiness, harder to ignore or dismiss the more prolonged the endurance.

For George, confronting fears was a lifelong skill acquired over many years: taking the knocks, making ill-judged decisions and not learning from past errors, all served to muddy the waters. Making the harder calls on personal and career transitions seemed to open up a chasm of doubt in his mind, but with the right support and a leap of faith in his own abilities, the challenges that lay ahead of him became as alluring as a late spring sunset after a rain-soaked day.

MOOSE CONQUERING FEAR

Avoiding a fear can become a full time occupation, which can overtake a life in an all-consuming manner, but combatting it can release a calm, which overcomes the severest of circumstances and allows a life to be lived freely.

A la Recherche du Soulagement

George's early years were often couched in confronting and combatting fears.

If allowed to dominate, they have the potential to derail an entire life or subvert real potential, beneath a shroud of latent, rising misgivings that can preoccupy and distract from the enjoyment of a fulfilling coexistence with others.

Simple occurrences or one bad experience – as he well knew – could turn uneasiness into a lasting fear.

For him this took different forms: an underarm aching suddenly when being shouted at or reprimanded by a manager; limbs seizing up in front of lowered heads of geese (an image only too readily and vividly recalled); stomach twisted and lips quivering in an outburst of fear and anger that a father is about to strike out at a mother, where protective instincts are laid bare before an adult in a temper. That is never a safe place for one of tender years to go, but a necessary almost primeval instinct kicks in to restore the balance of a peaceful home.

For George, finding an antidote to these seemed like a life's work with not enough hours in a day to address them all.

So he decided to tackle these and other fears one at a time.

Too Many Teeth

'I hate the dentist' is a not uncommon sentiment shared among many children and adults alike.

For George, this fear was compounded by having a second set of milk teeth!

The all too frequent visits to Ms Smith's dental asylum were the bane of this seven to ten year old's life. He could recall it in all its intensity at a moment's notice and could recite it by heart to anyone willing to listen:

> Her frame was larger than most that I'd encountered: an imposing figure not to be crossed. The black floorboards – worn back in places to the bare wood over decades I suppose with gaps in them clearly visible – creaked… even under a child's weight. The rocking horse, just as worn out as the floorboards, sat incongruously still. From my viewpoint on top of the patent leather seats, it did not stir. Curiously, it never gave the impression of having been ridden at any point in its past, nor of having given joy to any child attending that practice. Its threadbare mane made it look old before its time. My sight blurs as my name is called and the butterflies turn to knots in my stomach, as I am told to sit upright on the black dentist's chair. The indistinct conversation in the background is irrelevant. There is no discussion to be had. "They have to come out." The most odious rubber bung placed between the teeth serves two purposes: firstly, it keeps your mouth open once you've gone under – *sleep* is not in any way an appropriate term for that dazed and dizzying nightmare by the way – secondly, it prevents you from biting your tongue… so she said. I didn't believe that. The bung was a painful reminder, as it reeked of the gas (nitrous oxide) that was about to be unleashed on you. Being told it was called *laughing gas* didn't help matters. Slipping under, I saw concentric circles appear before me, deepening with every repeated turn of those brown spirals, dragging me in deeper, the cream lines around them fuzzy, like electrically charged edges. The last time I had to have it, I was told by my concerned mother afterwards "You nearly didn't come out of that one!" I hated it. Loathed the place and its secret work, hidden from street view

and no help in sight once inside, no recourse to a mother's loving hug to take away the fear.

When injections replaced that awful practice of using gas, the sharp jab was also a discomfort, but far less so than the previous method. He was grateful for that advancement, but equally determined to find a way of suppressing this pain and the anticipation of the fear of the pain, before it became a permanent feature of his life. He understood that to keep his teeth healthy, this had to be endured every six months, but there had to be a better way.

Years later, George would be in a position to cope with this and even look forward to going for check-ups. So much so, that he stayed with his regular dentist for more than twenty-eight years.

Decades later, George would also read research stating the disadvantages of using gas, including not using it on those with lung conditions such as his and warning of the consequences of misuse or overuse. He stirred uneasily in his seat as he read that, grateful again that this was in the distant past and that both he and dentistry had moved on.

A Water Baby

Another burgeoning fear of his was water. This was not limited to the seemingly genetic aversion to the very first wash time, instilled in every young boy ever conceived. This extended well into his teenage years, possibly after several adverse encounters with that medium. These included unverifiable wanderings off course as an infant into his back garden pond, as well as falling through ice on the blacksmith's pond opposite his house, while going to retrieve a makeshift ice puck from a hole in the ice. They couldn't have helped. It was also an ironic twist that he, an Aquarian, should suffer most from this embarrassing fear, uppermost in his mind as he lowered himself gingerly into the icy waters of the nearby town's outdoor swimming pool for another unwelcome lesson.

'Come on George! Let go of the side and just push off!'

'I could say the same to you, sir.' muttered George imperceptibly. 'Just push off and leave me alone', he said through gritted teeth, while wrestling with the imponderable contradiction between the science of things floating naturally and a body that always wants to sink.

Viewing the other boys half way across, arriving all too quickly at the other side, made his heart sink lower. The humiliation of it hung round his neck like a life ring with a slow puncture. In spite of asking the closest of friends what their secret was, the answer was always an unhelpful 'It's simple. Just push off from the side and swim.'

It was easy for them. 'Lucky are they,' he pondered resentfully, with more than a hint of jealousy, 'who get to learn in much warmer waters.' He had come to assign special powers of flotation to those more fortunate than himself, who used to holiday in exotic locations such as the Mediterranean and Australia.

His parents had always joked about their honeymoon *abroad*, which for them meant the Isle of Wight. Well it was good enough for Queen Victoria – her favourite location apparently – but clearly this was not a viable solution for George. He doubted very much that the waters there were much warmer than the North Sea, since they were all connected, weren't they!

This continued throughout his big school days until he was sixteen. A change came about borne of necessity which, as he had been taught, was the mother of invention. George was no stranger to inventions. He fabricated excuses on many occasions for missing swimming lessons, but this was no new invention. People, after all, had been swimming for thousands of years, hadn't they?

The solution presented itself, or rather himself, in the person of his sister's boyfriend, who kindly offered to help him to swim. The need was clear and impending. An upcoming trip to France was planned and George, a keen student of the language, was damned if he was going to miss out on that chance. He was to become a *moniteur* to younger children in a *colonie de vacances* for two weeks. One of the main features and major attractions was the canal, which ran close to its perimeter. He was told that the canal was fifty metres wide and, as the boyfriend pointed out,

'If you can swim twenty-five metres, I'll credit you with the good sense to swim to the nearest bank, should you fall in.' George's more than sound maths schooling bore this out and so they began.

The remarkable point was that it was just a simple change in perspective that turned the whole thing around for him. Instead of viewing his approach as having to jump on top of the water and somehow magically float, the focus was on starting below the water level and floating up to the surface. They started by dunking heads in the water and holding their breath while doing so, then repeating the same dunking, but this time blowing out air underwater. This effectively put control of the experience back in George's hands. He knew it did not take much strength to blow out underwater and it allowed his body to relax. When pushing off from the side underwater, he just let the water do its thing and he floated quickly to the surface. Brilliant!

Why he hadn't thought of it, he could not say, but he was so grateful to put that behind him. Looking back on it, he thought his fear probably started with shampoo making its way inexorably down the side of his head and into his eyes, during those to-be-avoided hair washing ceremonies at home. Kneeling down next to the bath and having dipper loads of mixed warm, hot and cold water poured over his head as a child was, he thought, at least partly responsible.

He put that aside now, signed up for the trip and on his first outing onto the canal, took the helm of a two-man dinghy and experienced the unforgettable and exhilarating pull of the wind in the sails.

Going the Extra 250 Miles

Subsequently at university – with that particular fear cast aside – this new appreciation for all things watery extended to being part of a coxless four, trying his luck in a single skull and kayaking up the river at dusk. Disembarking several hundreds of metres upstream to hunker down beside the glowing fires of the watering hole, known as the Rose Tree, was immensely rewarding. The return, just after 11pm, was nothing short of magical. He took the lead over his two companions and in the stillness their conversation ceased with the same amazement. His prow was the only tip breaking the glass-like surface of the river, at peace with the world it seemed after a hard day, now flowing effortlessly downstream. They took turns to lead and chat returned, only when the lights of the towpath and city were in view and movements of life could be seen from afar. They returned to their shared lodging and slept like the proverbial logs.

Being three – shortly to become four in their second year billeted in the same digs – there was a more than fair chance of one of them having to rise early for the almost inevitable 9am lecture.

'I'm sure they do it deliberately', moaned Leo in an unusual moment of disillusionment, in what was otherwise an immensely rewarding union of like minds and interests. He was George's regular companion on the walk down the steep slope to the footbridge across the river, before flattening out on the way to the Modern Languages building, as they both studied French as their main subject. A mane of medium-length, curly, fair hair and an unshaven appearance gave Leo the look of a foreign gentleman. Most who did comment, thought him to hail from the Iberian peninsula. 'Good job I'm studying Spanish then.' he quipped, on our first real working week. George had opted for a more challenging second language. He could find only the Cyrillic alphabet on offer, facilitated by the university's home grown Russian course with all language books authored by his tutor. 'I'd probably have chosen Chinese as the most obscure of all,' George quipped back, 'but it wasn't on the list.'

The Iron Curtain was firmly down at that time, with no access to visit that country, even for the Honours students of the day. They had to be content with slides, articles and translated texts to begin to appreciate its culture, but in truth barely scratching the surface of that vast continent.

Many decades later, when George eventually went to Russian-speaking countries before the motherland herself, he would be asked by more than one old woman travelling on the same bus, 'Why Russian… at that time?' His response he remembered from these same university days verbatim 'Well, I knew the curtain wouldn't be there for ever and when it came down, I wanted to be among the first to take advantage.'

What he went on to say – in his now fractured language – was that he did not account for the loss of vocabulary over time, to the point that he knew these word sounds in Russian without knowing their meaning anymore. The old ladies helped him out there and were very warm in welcoming him to their fascinating country. All new countries George encountered were fascinating for the same reason: new language to grasp, a few words of politeness and thankfulness, a new culture to understand on the ground and not from the forty thousand foot view of temporal commentators giving in to easy assessments under publishing deadlines.

Russia, however, was different: like meeting an old friend he hadn't seen in decades and extremely glad to renew his acquaintance, albeit for the briefest of stays. 'The people make it,' he would say on more than one occasion, 'they always do.'

The two of them tramped the red-tiled, uneven surface of the pavements, dodging the many puddles accumulating in the broken slabs, in their open-toed sandals, rugby shorts, blue horizontally striped tee shirts and French beret… naturally. How else were they to remember which course they were on and go to the right lectures!

The building itself was fairly unprepossessing, its dark brown bricks reminiscent of those put up in the 1980s in a rush to fulfil an urgent need. Its one, perhaps two, saving graces were the view from the tutors' rooms of the river, which were awe-inspiring in themselves, and secondly the multiple glass doors which guarded its entrance. The balcony seating on the first floor formed the holding area pre-lectures. From a privileged position kneeling up on the couch, you could see clearly the approach of everyone else into and out of the building.

It was on such a blue sky day, that they both had arrived early for their 9am lecture. These would always be packed with around sixty students. On this morning they noticed that there was a hastily written notice stuck on two out of four doors which read 'No Entry – Door Closed'. The same thought occurred to both and they rushed hurriedly up the stairs after the deed was done to see the fruits of their labours.

They did not have to wait long. Within seconds, the first student saw the notices, chose another door and found it to be locked. So they chose the one remaining door which surely would let them in, only to find that it did not. It then became a study in psychology to test people's reactions and time to correctly assess the situation before them.

Some laughed hysterically, others giggled, one or two alpha males became overtly annoyed, partly from their extended hangovers deceiving their eyes and playing havoc with their remaining senses, until it became 'No joke!' Fortunately they were rescued by a female of the species, who had not had as much to drink as they had. The two protagonists were by this time completely incapable of anything but incontrollable mirth, which redoubled every time the sound of a locked glass door being tried rose up to the balcony seating above. A few interested onlookers waiting for the same lecture made their way to their vantage position and joined in with raucous laughter.

'That'll teach them to be awake in the morning.' George cackled, while pausing between shoulders lifting and stomach aching with laughter.

'Ah, there's at last a decent citizen.' Leo espied a more auspicious-looking young woman mounted the steps leading up to the doors purposefully and, having seen the chaos from a distance, took one notice down and placed it back on the correct door. Not wishing to spoil people's fun, she thoughtfully did not interfere with the other notice, so the fun could continue.

'Idle minds!' the tutor echoed in the waiting area, before calling them all in for another riveting session on linguistics.

'Lessons in life rather', mused George to himself, before exchanging knowing glances with Leo. He somehow knew this would not be their last prank. Nor was it.

Any fear of moving 250 miles away from home was now a distant memory, as George's life began to open up before him with what he felt would be lasting friendships and fun times, which would live on long in the collective memory of them all.

The Three Stooges

The third member of this newly formed clan, Stuart, hailed from near Stamford Bridge which – as he had to educate his ignorant southerner roommates – lies to the east of York and not in a borough of London. His accent was welcoming, issuing as it did from beneath an untidy mass of fair curly hair atop a smaller, but "perfectly formed, fine figure of a man" as he would often remind them. His face beamed with a full set of teeth accompanied by an insuppressible, habitual snigger at the slightest amusement. This bade well for them all, since they all agreed from the outset that laughter was the best medicine to get them through the next three or four years.

'Have you noticed,' said Stuart after our first excursion to the dining hall, 'how young they all are?'

'Well, we are a year older than them', replied Leo. 'Yes, but just twelve months. How can twelve months make such a difference?' insisted Stuart. 'Have you heard them too?'

'I haven't been listening in on their conversations intently.' suggested George, trying to instil some sort of social etiquette that might be appropriate. They both shot him down.

'You've got to be kidding me!' they both said in unison. 'They're still talking about A levels and school as though they were important now', added Leo.

'They have had the whole summer to forget, I suppose,' George recovered slightly, 'but give them time. They will come round in good time.'

This was unsurprising to the three of them on further discussion, as they discovered they had all taken a year out. This was either due to delaying entry because of Oxbridge applications, taking a rest from academic work to earn some money or a combination of both. From their early days together the other two deduced that, in Stuart's case, it was more likely that he'd missed the application deadline by oversleeping too many times.

It was quickly agreed that they would have to have a means of communicating between them, which the rest of their year group could not possibly decipher. So it was, that an entire afternoon and early evening were spent devising a numbered list of codes, before a single assignment was even contemplated.

Moose Conquering Fear

It is beyond the bounds of propriety and the residual long term memory to recall all such codes. Sufficient to say some of them were rude, some aimed at both sexes without preferential treatment and others added as a result of received experience, which they all thought highly comical and worthy of immediate inclusion. These were referred to individually as "a number N job", where the number N related to an A4 cheat code list, which they shared among each other and updated regularly.

Three such examples, appearing well down the list at numbers 18-20, were taken from the many gatherings, which took place during freshers' week. These were aimed to balance interactions of large numbers of people, provided with little food but much more by way of alcoholic refreshment. They failed.

Hence were borne from calamity rather than necessity the following:

No. 18: a mid-sentence job

No. 19: a mid-paragraph job and

No. 20: a mid-story job

You could be the deliverer or the recipient of them all, but more frequently it meant – for our intrepid three adventurers – being deserted in the middle of their attempt to engage another human being or beings with an account, amusing anecdote or an opinion which was rejected out of hand. Utterly demoralising for anyone wishing to engage socially, but fortunately for these three it was laughable and became the butt of their coded in-joke system, reserved for their ears only.

Leo referred to the three of them now as the three stooges, a title lost on the other two, who had no clue what he was talking about. It wasn't as though studies, extra-curricular sport and leisure activities would ever permit them to read up on the reference. So it was forgotten till much later. All they needed to understand was that it was a comedy with three main characters.

Gills Perch

Like any good comedy, this one had its farcical setting and its own running joke.

The three had been billeted – or consigned or confined, they were not sure which, to begin with – to a set of rooms in a three-floor terraced house, which sat in a row of houses at the top of an extraordinary road. It ran steeply downhill for about four hundred metres, every dwelling abutted against the next all the way to the bottom, where an enormous wooden buttress construction – probably from Victorian times from its simplicity – struggled to keep all the other houses from falling over.

They renamed the whole street 'Gills Perch' because of the precarious position their house seemed to occupy, perched as it was above a busy road no more than thirty metres away.

The short cut to the college was accessed through a downstairs bathroom glazed door. The door led out onto a concrete slab patio, held up by a two-deep slab construction, angled at 30° to the vertical and bulging in the middle, as if the patio had eaten too much. From there down some uneven steps, through a small garden past an ageing and uncared-for apple tree and out through another man-sized door in a red brick wall which towered over them, twice their height and serving no other purpose than to limit the traffic noise. That failed too.

The rooms were adequate they thought. Small enough to swing a cat in, with a small gas fire now filling what used to be a bedroom hearth – on which they could and did bake marshmallows as an experiment, once – a single bed, matching single wardrobe and no desk. Off George's room was another tiny closet, where a single bed and wardrobe just fitted in. That was Stuart's chosen independence from the main room and where large parts of his day were spent. George didn't like to knock on his door, so as not to disturb him. Four weeks into term, when asked if he was going down to breakfast, the response was

'Hey you two, do you realise, I've missed two 9am lectures this week and that is 40% of my course!' It was to be Stuart's own running joke and he did wonder, on more than one occasion, how his life may be affected in future by these five solitary hours a week that were meant to transform his life. Stuart was a deep thinker… and often said as much.

Compared with the other two's 19-20 hours a week on a language or two, he felt it oddly curious and slightly inexplicable how studying three subjects could leave his lot so impoverished, as it clearly was. He guessed it was the curse of the 'ology degrees, which he had succumbed to. What seemed a good idea at the time was now wreaking havoc with his intended future aspirations: that of joining the Hong Kong police force 'Because,' he claimed in his own words at that time, 'they are the most corrupt police force in the world, according to the articles I have read.'

'Ah ok, so that's why you're studying Sociology and Anthropology, is it?' quizzed Leo as he winked at George. He could not remember the other 'ology and so missed it off the list. They both agreed he was a funny guy, in the nicest possible way.

The main feature of the house though was not the threadbare carpets throughout – though none of their parents would have tolerated them – it was the staircase. It reminded George of the sixth form trip he had taken to Blackpool with twenty or so other boys. Having whizzed up and down the Grand National roller coaster, they ended up in a combination of rooms, all designed to rattle your senses in one way or another. There were convex and concave mirrors, steps which broke in the middle, rose and fell at different times or cross beams which alternated up and down, anything to upset your balance.

The stairs in Gills Perch, as it was now affectionately known, were obviously designed by the same architect as that fun fair attraction. The minute you set foot on the first flight, your whole body weight was slung to one side towards the outer wall, similar to the spiral steps you'd encounter in a castle fortress, but without the rope to assist you on the inside.

George came to the conclusion – being of a practical mind which he credited to his engineer father – that the best and simplest approach was part mental and part physical. You had to have trust firstly in the stairs and that nothing was going to collapse. Secondly, you had to use your weight and lower your centre of gravity to swing round the corners, like the hammer or discus is circled round and round till the moment of release at the top of the stairs, when you would be flung into your room.

So much for the setting, but there was one final curiosity which gave rise to another running joke and that was the downstairs sunken room, which was first encountered when opening the door. The whole house sat three steps below the street level. The more observant passer-by would not miss the sunken front window in winter, with the lamp blazing out of it from the fourth year student, who had already taken up residence there before they arrived.

'He must have his own bathroom.' Stuart and George suspected, as they had not seen hide nor hair of him in or around their shared bathroom on the first floor above. George wasted no time in introducing them to the fellow resident, who went by the name of Jim: curious chap with a beard and quite a shock of dark, curly and wavy hair, which concealed much of his head. They thought he came from the Home Counties, though they never found out which one. His door was sunken too. Picking their way over creaking floorboards, they walked the corridor past his room, knocking on his door with a loud shout of 'Jim!' Regardless of the frequency of the prank, it always solicited the familiar and habitual response: 'Yup!' immediately followed by them running up the stairs in an exercise more in futility than malice, which Jim took in good part.

Running and Rowing

Into this mix was added a fourth personality in a certain Gerry, who arrived fresh out of school during their second year. They concluded that last year's intake was an unfortunate one-off, since the newly installed Gerry was both worldly-wise and amusing in equal parts. He also helped them all live a healthier lifestyle than in their first year, because he was a keen runner. As both Leo and George were keen on sport and had established places in college rugby and hockey clubs respectively, they cheerfully accepted the challenge to rise every morning during the week and go for a run. This activity was completely lost on Stuart, who loved his bed more than life itself.

No ordinary run was theirs either. Skittling on down the slope to the river, they followed its course round in a semi-circle before encountering Tonks Hill. This was a notoriously steep climb, which wound upwards across tree roots, rich dark slippery earth, in between young holly trees trying to vie with the long-term beech residents for sunlight and moisture. Emerging onto a flat part at its summit, a glance over the shoulder glimpsed the magnificence of the cathedral before continuing on. That was the most telling climb and major punisher of over-excessive nights out. From there, it gave out onto the other main drag of colleges, strewn on one side of the road or the other down a gentle slope, coming as it did as an extended warm down of two or so miles, before a sprint finish along the river bank to the footbridge. A total of five miles certainly did the trick: not only encouraging less overindulgence the night before during the week, but also guaranteeing a super early start to the day. With the three of them running together, there would always be one of them, who was keener than the other two and duly rousted them out of bed with no excuses.

Suitably energised, 9am lectures became a breeze and coping with workload and balancing sporting commitments suddenly became tolerable and, what's more to the point, enjoyable.

In fact their repertoire extended outwards to tennis for them all – George's first time on a court made him curse the day other school sports got in the way of trying out for tennis – to college team badminton for George and to rowing for them all too.

Up first for rowing was Leo. 'I'll show you how it's done.' he said proudly and somewhat annoyingly smugly, 'I used to row at a senior school down in Kent.'

Stuart and George exchanged knowing glances. 'This should be interesting', Stuart said leaning towards George's ear, so as not to be overheard.

Perhaps unwisely, Leo chose to give his demonstration in a single skull. It is likely that the other boats were out, as it was a gloriously sunny afternoon and not a lecture or essay in sight.

'So this is how you get in…' Leo said as he positioned one oar sensibly on the floating jetty with the other at right angles sitting delicately on the water's surface. 'Now just lower yourself gently into the boat like so…'

'So far, so good' and other words of cautious approval met with Leo's appreciation, as he pushed gently away from the side, resting the other oar on the riverbank side of the water. He was barely two metres out when he attempted the first stroke with both oars. One caught the water at perfect right angles on the other side, while the nearside oar caught an enormous crab, went scything straight to the bottom and the whole skull turned turtle and Leo was gone.

The two spectators roared with laughter as a bedraggled Leo stood up in the shallows, soaked to the skin but with an enormous tooth-filled smile beaming out at them. Accompanied by a prolonged snigger, he joined in with the hilarity.

'Well, that's not quite how I remember it!' he managed, pulling the skull and oars to the side, for his companions to help get them out of the water. Thankfully it didn't take long for his clothes to dry on the walk back and a warm bath took away any residual injured pride.

The Bollard Tree

As the ride at the Grand National roller coaster in Blackpool during his last school year's prefect team trip had proved, George had been blissfully unaware of the fear of heights, which can strike at any age. His demand to be let out at the top of a Ferris wheel ride – while it paused to allow more people to climb aboard – didn't really count, as he relied on others' collective memory rather than his own, being of a very young age at the time.

He had found the Blackpool ride exhilarating, but the ride left precious little time to contemplate the heights it reached before plunging him down the other side. So that did not really count either.

What was needed was that skill to be put to the test. Of course he had not set out with anything particular in mind, but it came to the three stooges at the same time during a restful early summer's afternoon spent sitting on the paving slab patio.

Before them, the previously sorrowful apple tree had been decorated by themselves after many outings to local hostelries. Multiple units of beer later, their excursions tended to culminate in an early morning return in high spirits, scouring the landscape for a suitable souvenir to take back to the house. On most occasions a lonely bollard – abandoned by workmen weeks before and now having grass and bindweed forcing its way up the centre and protruding from any available hole or gash in its side – was crying out for attention and called out to them to be rescued. They were glad to oblige.

It would have been impractical to have stored them on the stairs or in their rooms – clearly not a step willingly taken, to avoid incriminating themselves – so their collective decision was to breathe new life into the apple tree. It no longer bore any meaningful fruit, but its shoots seemed invigorated when they adorned it with different coloured bollards. Yellow ones, green, blue on occasions and of course the ubiquitous red and orange ones too. It had the look of a Christmas tree and of being loved all year round.

'Do you think we should put those back some day?' suggested Stuart casually, helping himself to another beer and trying to put another missed lecture behind him.

The Bollard Tree

'Nah, don't think so. We went to a lot of trouble for those...' Leo responded briskly and George added '... and the tree would look so bare without them. But it is quite a collection. What, there must be over a dozen there now.'

'Perhaps we could find another use for them before the end of term,' George said, thinking aloud, 'some higher purpose.'

'That's it,' shouted Leo at the top of his voice, 'of course, why didn't we think about it sooner. Time to make plans.'

Everyone knew the Principal, because he made a point of speaking with candidates at interview, or shortly upon arrival, and was well-respected among the student body.

The Vice-Principal however was a different proposition. Quite diminutive in size, he hailed from the valleys of Wales, but did not seem to exhibit the finer points of that country. He neither sang nor was of a smiling or irrepressible disposition, but rather sullen in expression with never a good word to say about students. Privately, he may have considered them to be a scourge on society, or so it seemed to our intrepid trio. They thought he perhaps did not like his job.

Their engagement with him had been minimal, as they left each other alone to go about their separate lives, but all that was about to change.

On an increasingly warm night in late May, the three had spent more than a goodly portion of their evening visiting some familiar haunts, beginning under the arches of the viaduct to start the beer rolling. To increase the efficiency of such a night, they were diligent in finding enough establishments within the normal city radius, to limit walking between them to a hundred metres or less. This included popping into the aptly named Travellers' Rest, renowned in their own eyes not only for the tasty tipple served up but also for the opportunity to hear the slightly affected, higher-pitched voice of one of their waiters, who proclaimed 'Two soups!' to the amusement of them all. They would often order the same between three of them on Sunday lunchtime, just to hear that order and would often delay their acknowledgment of it, so it would be repeated. It did not sound the same if there were three soups.

Their evening drew to a close deliberately late, choosing the local bar opposite their lodgings to take part in what they had witnessed almost every night of every week: the then traditional lock-in. They stayed on till the small hours and crossed the road, entering their digs quietly so as not to disturb Jim... for once.

'Come on,' said Leo, 'go and put something dark on. That pink shirt's no good Stuie!'

'Okay. See you out back in five. No need to synchronise watches.' came the reply.

Out through the bathroom door they sidled and into the garden.

'Imagine what it would be like,' George mused, 'we could carry four each over the road in the dead of night and make our way up quickly through the empty car park. Pausing, as we notice a light in the small corner window – which we assume to be the stairs inside – we would huddle up against the light brown stones by the entrance: the one only allowed for administrative staff and the Vice-Principal. Clambering up onto the porch parapet, we could hand up each cone, clamber up to the roof from there and place one on each of those protruding lead cowlings. Must be heating outlets I guess. Wouldn't that be awesome?'

'Fantastic… and if we have one left over – perhaps the yellow no parking traffic cone – we could put it up on top of the flagpole for good measure.' added Leo, to the great delight of the other two.

'Yes,' said Stuie, 'but I'd have to pass on that last one, as you'll need to be extra tall and stand on tip toe to get anywhere near it.'

The three of them retired to their beds excited at the prospect of the next day but succumbing inevitably to slumber, which their exhausted bodies craved above all else.

They were late down to breakfast in the morning. Luckily it was a Saturday… but not just any Saturday. For today was College Day!

A yearly event hotly anticipated by the whole student body in both colleges who participated. There were marquees in the grounds, special service in the chapel to kick things off for some, special buffet lunch to feast on for others, fun and games on the immaculately mown grass banks overlooking the fabulous prospect across the river, through mature blossomed trees to the university cricket fields beyond. A sight for sore eyes indeed! Even more so for the Vice-Principal, whose job it was to organise such events, to ensure they all go smoothly.

His first task of the day, like his daily schedule, would not normally be shared with students but today was different. His face was tinged slightly red as he marched down the lawns to the small groups assembled on disparate coloured blankets, spread out on the grass with glasses and wine at the ready. He spoke to anyone who would listen, but curiously solicited no response. As he drew nearer to the small group of six that our three belonged to, his annoyance could be plainly heard.

'Well, do you see? Do you know anything about that?'

'About what sir?' two of them enquired.

'Do you not see it? If it were up to me, I'd have them handed over to the police. They will pay for this… dearly! I'll not have it, I swear to it.'

The perplexed expressions on their faces escaped his notice, as it was customary for the Vice-Principal not to look at anyone and certainly not directly at them. Off he strode to another group to repeat his protestations yet again and, only through the slight variation of his delivery and gesticulations, did they ascertain what he was in so much disquiet about.

With some consummate finger-pointing, he stretched out his arm at an approximate angle of 40-45° in their estimation to the college roof. There, emblazoned for all to see, were bollard adornments of every variety dotted along the roof to celebrate the day, with the pinnacle being magnificently displayed on top of the flagpole.

'A dream come true.' gasped George to an enthralled audience. Their eyes were fixed on the unique spectacle, which they somehow knew would be recorded in college history and retold by many as doting grandparents, regaling their grandchildren with tales of when they were at college. 'Oh what fun!' came one response from a satisfied onlooker. 'Hilarious', 'Amazing' and other more extreme, unrepeatable remarks followed.

With it being a weekend, nothing changed and as surely as the sun rose over the May ornamental cherry tree blossom in the coming days, so the spectacular sight remained in full view of the rest of the university. The student grapevine did the rest.

It was towards the end of the following week that a rather formal notice appeared on headed notepaper in the Junior Common Room and in other public places around the college. The initial annoyance was plain to see, but soon fell into ridiculous rhetoric on how the Vice-Principal had had to employ a contractor – an above average height individual – to scale the roof and remove the offending bollards at the princely cost of £30. The note emphasised:

> This amount will be recouped from the daring individuals who were responsible for this reckless act.
>
> Furthermore, I will expect those same individuals to report to my office at their earliest convenience.
>
> The Vice-Principal

'Well, of course, any self-respecting Vice-Principal would know that students would be far too busy with lectures, essay and seminar preparation to find any time free for such a meeting.' stated George in a matter-of-fact manner.

'Goodness, is that the time?' said Leo, 'It's Friday. We must be going, otherwise we'll miss the bar quiz!' The other two laughed out loud.

Now the bar at college could not have been expected to be plush by any stretch of the imagination. It lived up to its billing. There were no lounging sofas, easy chairs or bright open vistas onto the slopes and plains below, looking out over the river. Oh no. The moment you crossed the threshold, you knew you were in a bar. Not because of the gaudy yellow décor or hard wooden seats, but the soles of your feet stuck to the floor as you walked in. Every step required several newtons of force to lift up the outer sole with an accompanying ripping sound, as if the bottom of the shoe had been forcibly removed. No one could therefore enter quietly. Everyone turned their heads at that sound to see who might have wandered in… calling out to them to get the next round in.

'Hey Leo, George, Stuie. Come on over. We've saved you a place!' came the open invitation from the sporting fraternity corner. Their table tops were already hidden beneath empty pint glasses, with one or two leaning precariously against one another for support and in clear danger of toppling onto the black and white chequered Formica floor. 'Here, let me clear some of these away,' said George, whose turn it was to serve behind the bar, 'make a bit more room for you thirsty lads.'

Returning behind the bar always made him smile as he read the notice on the back of one of the draught lager taps, which said very simply in capital letters, as a warning to all who poured or drank it: ROCKET FUEL.

The evening came and went. The quiz results were largely ignored and the three retired in the direction of their rooms, while discussing the imminent opportunity.

They thought about the best way to reply to the VP's missive, not just for themselves, but also to find a way to preserve the rights of students everywhere to do some mad things occasionally. So long as it hurt nobody or did not damage property – that was their unwritten creed – when playing pranks on others and each other, they saw no harm in it.

Although many found the VP's attitude annoying, it was also vaguely amusing that he took to pen and paper. People, they thought, who took life too seriously should be tolerated in small doses… and in his case, extra small doses!

The following note was left on the VP's office door:

> Sorry to have missed you. We did call round as you requested, but could not find you in.
>
> From: the daring individuals

Pinned to the door at 3:30am, that seemed most unlikely. There was no follow up meeting and they could only imagine how disappointed, not to mention how beside himself, he may have been at that news. The matter was promptly dropped.

The Group of Six

Regardless of other fears encountered and overcome, George still grappled clumsily with the knotty problem of girls. Everyone expected you to have had a girlfriend before coming to university or be actively pursuing one while there. Neither of these was true unfortunately.

It wasn't just the 'girlfriend thing', but more of the 'sex thing'. Having taken a year out, he was now fast approaching his 20th birthday with no clue of how to go about it or what it entailed. This hugely embarrassing situation was harder to cover up and when conversations erred on the smutty side, he shuffled awkwardly in his seat or looked away momentarily, hoping the spotlight would not return to him.

Thankfully it wasn't too long before the act was committed and he could breathe a little more easily. 'Is that's what it's all about? Really?' he thought to himself the morning after. 'Surely there's more to it than that. Why does everybody go on about it so much?' He could not comprehend what all the fuss was about. He had tried to stifle a tumultuous 'Is that it?' on the night, but kept himself from saying it out loud. No offence to the person he had got to know that evening. She was a pleasant, good-looking girl and he surely didn't deserve the gift she was about to bestow on an otherwise undistinguished, frankly non-existent, sexual encounter career.

She and her redheaded companion frequented the bar quite often – they had that in common for sure. They talked openly for a couple of hours and were so engrossed in each other's company, that they both missed her friend and his two buddies having left a while before.

It seemed very cosy in his room with the gas fire lit, its red bars and blue and yellow flames dancing up the hearth and on the face in front of him. He could feel the warmth of the fire hot on his face, as they began to embrace more fully. The single bed afforded not a lot of room once his six foot body was under the covers, but they managed with some laughter, as first the red flimsy knitted blanket and then his own clumsiness got in the way of any kind of passionate, film-surpassing or mind-obliterating embrace.

He found the target eventually with some help and slumped down with relief, as much due to the excessive alcohol, which threatened his evening conclusion, as his exertion in the act.

The Group of Six

Both were covered by the red blanket when his roommate Stuie stumbled in, passed their bed and into his broom cupboard bedroom. By the time Stuie rose, she was gone… and then the questions started.

This time, at least he had some idea of what went on, but kept the discussion short and did not give any details, which were private and somewhat embarrassing too. George was greeted by her companion at lunch with a cheery, rhetorical 'Who was a naughty boy last night…' He smiled awkwardly and moved on with his tray to a different table. He felt sure he had not 'performed' as such. When he met his first again, they exchanged politenesses in a friendly manner, but both sensed relief that things would not be taken any further.

With that episode squarely behind him, George decided that perhaps it would be best to just accumulate some female friends, in the hope that one may take more than a passing interest in him.

His studies helped him in this. Although most of his French set were a year younger than both himself and Leo, it became clear that the old adage that girls mature faster than boys was self-evident in the conversations he now had with them. It helped that he was among only five boys in a set of over sixty students: this was the reason why it was said that the French set always teamed up with the Engineering set, when putting on combined discos, to balance the numbers.

George didn't have to wait for that occasion, before encountering an amusing little woman called Louise. He used the term woman advisedly, as she seemed wise beyond her years, a phrase which had been used about him at home and a reason for him being drawn unexpectedly to her. She was tiny by comparison, cute, natural with straight, light brown hair, which looked as if it had been poured sparingly over her head – a treasure in itself. She wore mostly long-flowing skirts, down to her sensible shoes and almost always topped with a thick-weave pebbledash jumper, like staring into the gravel at the bottom of a beautifully clear, chalkscape stream. The print-style skirts gave the impression of a much older woman in a young body. He was taken with her and knew from the outset that they would be firm friends.

It wasn't long before they were talking about their own companions and as it turned out, Louise had two companions of her own in Berenice and Harriet. 'Wow, that's great', said George, 'Why don't we all get together tonight for a chat and a drink?'

'Sounds good.' agreed Lou, as she now insisted on being called.

Feeling like they'd been set up on a blind date to begin with, the other two, Leo and Stuie, were reluctant to come along, but the absence of sports training that evening, a chance of making new female friends and most tellingly of all, no cash in hand, meant that they were persuaded.

'How do people survive at Uni when they run out of cash in their second year?' Stuie pondered, not really anticipating an answer.

'No idea.' George replied, 'When mine runs out that's it. There's no more, nor would I expect there to be more.'

'Well that's true,' hesitated Leo, 'but if push comes to shove, I could always give home a call to alleviate our situation.' Though not immediately in a dire situation, all three recognised the fall back and breathed a little more easily. However, tonight was not one of those 'going-out-and-getting-blotto' nights, so they took up George's invitation to meet three delightful young ladies, as they turned out to be.

Sitting down in the Junior Common Room – or JCR as it was more efficiently known – had its advantages later in the day. Relatively few students passed that way – perhaps the odd one or two checking out sports notices, teams or events – but generally no throngs and there was no bar there, which made it economically attractive.

Lou introduced Berenice, in height not too dissimilar from herself, had thicker hair, longer, down to the middle of her back, loose and impeccably groomed. She wore a thinner jumper, cashmere it seemed like, and tight jeans accentuating her neat and adequately fulsome rear. Her hair swished around when she turned to face anyone, hiding the smooth contours of her face at the sides, much to her detriment. She had an engaging smile and a happy, though cautious disposition. George had estimated that she was perhaps recovering from a fairly recent split in a relationship or maybe was just sensibly overcautious about all young men. He imagined her gran warning her before leaving for college of the tempestuous times that lay ahead and not to trust anything in trousers – not realising that the younger generation all wore trousers or jeans at that time – backed up admirably by the testaments of one or two concerned aunts. Then perhaps being given a more realistic view of life by a black sheep of the family, from the occasional wry smile and twinkly eye which lit up her face and the company she was with.

Next up was Harriet, who cut a much more demure figure. She was reserved and reticent, dressed in a more smart casual way, no doubt as instructed by her parents, who lived not too far away in Northumberland – a county of untold beauty as George would find out years later: a seaside devoid of fences to restrict adventuresome children from trying to run over the dunes and failing; village greens, where visiting Dads could play cricket considerately and freely with their sons and daughters. Her hair was fashioned naturally like a younger Sophia Loren but in light brown curls and waves, shaped in a circle around a well-proportioned, smooth-skinned face. There was also her coy smile, pushed out to the side whenever any one of the three boys cracked a joke or made a subtle reference to her most pleasing countenance.

It could well be said that when all three smiled together, the sun broke through and cast aside any misgivings or concerns of the day. It was this quality which was to endure through their three or four years at college together.

After that evening, it became clear they would be inseparable for most of their sojourn there. Just enjoying each other's company, without contemplating who would go out with whom, as it barely crossed their minds.

Of course Stuie began that topic as soon as they'd returned to their digs. Being the same size as the three girls – although Harriet would be a little taller and look down on the little fella – he felt he had more of a chance with one or two of them, but any advance made was glossed over as irrelevant in the grander scheme of things. They were friends.

Priory Pals

'Hey George, we were both wearing hooped rugby shirts. Do you think that's a sign? Do you think I have a chance with Lou?' snickered Stuie, squeezing air forcibly through half-clenched teeth – as he often did, giving the impression of a steam engine pulling out of the station – which brought a smile to all their faces.

'Not a chance,' replied George, 'she's far too sensible for that, ha-ha!'

'We all set?' asked Jim, who had suggested this trip in our first weeks there and within minutes of meeting our three new friends. 'Yep Jim, let's do it. We've got all the essentials', said George, brandishing two bags packed with wine bottles and nibbles for the six of them. Jim had kindly offered to drive them the two or three miles to a renowned beauty spot, where he sometimes came to take time out from his fourth year studies. He had arrived two to three weeks before them to start a Masters degree and both Stuie and George were glad to have an elder statesman to fall back on in those early days.

The girls had come prepared too. Jeans were the order of the day for any rough climbing encountered or uneven terrain. Lou's blue and white hoops with open neckline oozed comfort and did not match Stuie's faded dark green and orange hoops, as much as he'd have liked them to have done. Berenice had put her tresses in bunches for the occasion, sporting a blue matching top with bare arms, as if she had already rolled up her sleeves for the task ahead. Harriet turned out unmistakably as herself in jeans with a deep coral pink sweater, matching shoes and light brown shoulder bag, etched with coral pink writing.

Jim's thick white Arran jumper had probably given them a hint of the arduous walking ahead, so there was a deal of nervousness on the ride there. On disembarking, they were amazed to find a steep incline levelling out onto an idyllic location next to the river, where the ruins of a Benedictine Priory nestled gently on the luscious, well-maintained grass beneath.

'Why is it that monks always chose the best places?' George's question stemmed from photos he had seen of other abbeys and monasteries to the south of them, which seemed to have found a little corner of paradise to set up a haven from the world. 'Don't know,' answered Jim, 'but it wasn't just in this country. France has them too.' He continued, 'There used to live here a man called Goderic, who lived to a ripe old age – over a hundred years old, they think – and that's not bad for the 12th century, is it?'

They were glad to bow to Jim's superior knowledge, until they could find out more for themselves, or in George's case, discover a love of history which had eluded him from the age of twelve, when he gave it up as a bad job. As students of French, both Lou and George (and the absent Leo) couldn't wait for their third year abroad. None of them were to know then that two out of three would meet up over there during that year and did their own fair share of exploring that country and making new friends.

Their excitement was tempered though, since Berenice and Harriet would not be there when they returned, as they were both on a more normal three year course. 'Maybe we'll both end up doing a Masters like Jim and we could have an epic reunion', suggested Berenice. 'I think we'll end up having many reunions once we've left anyway.' added George.

They set about exploring the delight that is Finchale: walking under arches, between aisles of former religious contemplation, which had been first a hermitage and then a priory. A stone's throw away brought them to the clear babbling waters of the river's upper reaches, before it deepens and widens on its way into the city. On a warmer day they would have shed their footwear and paddled quite happily, but the sweaters were for a reason with autumn well advanced already. There was a definite crispness in the air.

That would not deter them though. Sitting down in the shelter of a grassy bank they broke out the snacks and drinks, settling down into easy, light and funny tales from times before their college journey had begun. Lou from Canterbury, Harriet from Northumberland and Berenice rather noncommittal about the exact location in the Home Counties, but it sounded very comfortable in the main.

'Did we forget the glasses?' enquired Harriet, in the hope that civilisation had not totally deserted them all, but to no avail. 'Oh no matter', Lou struck out boldly, taking the mouth of the bottle and putting it to her lips. Harriet, to everyone's surprise, followed suit with another wine bottle and snap, George's lens captured the moment just as Jim was about to do the same.

'Oh really?' she complained half-heartedly, 'I don't think that will make the papers!'

'It might do in Northumberland', quipped George, soliciting a wry smile from Harriet.

By the end of the afternoon, they were back in the city where the sun was now shielded by a veil of fog, which had descended like dry ice being poured into the river valley below, leaving the castle and part of the cathedral just visible on their shared promontory.

'This is still a truly magical place', mused George as he crossed the now almost deserted main road from their back garden to go into the dining room. He recalled vividly his arrival at the station for interview in February the year before, when heavy snow blanketed the ground, and in particular, the slope down from the station. With two large suitcases packed for just the three days, his first step was his last as he slid onto his backside, careering at pace to the bottom, followed shortly after by suitcases either side of him. Without getting up, he looked up to see the same vista of cathedral and castle in front of him and thought, 'This must be the place for me!'

Second Year Immersion

The second year is always a relief once it arrives. With first year exams passed and mandatory modules laid to rest, it is a time for focussing more in depth in your chosen areas of interest and potential expertise.

For George it had always been languages and immersing yourself in the culture, making new friends and trying new things. The immersion into cultures would not be satisfied until their third year abroad. The Modern Languages Society came a poor second, grateful though he was for the events organised to bring engineers and the French set together, again to balance out the sexes numerically.

Neither he nor Leo nor Stuie were particularly fond of wine or cheese, though they all three subscribed to Stuie's view expressed succinctly as 'I refuse nowt but blows, me!' in his distinctive Yorkshire, likeable lilt. They showed a clear preference – as most of their age group did at the time – for real ale, winter warmers in season and the occasional lager in the summer. In fact the only group they joined during freshers' week was CAMRA – the Campaign for Real Ale.

Nights out would often entail real ale bar crawls which, in a small city, were thoughtfully packed together, sometimes four or five to a street and even located in some reclusive spots, such as under the viaduct. Theirs was not so much a drink-immersed life, but it would be fair to say that it featured strongly enough to be not only a welcome distraction from their studies, but also put them all in a good mood... and their inebriation was wholly jovial and non-violent.

As their studies had long ingrained in them the need for exceptions to a rule – as well as in some cases to prove the rule – so it was that one particular birthday celebration started innocently enough, but was to cause them more than a passing headache in the following days to come.

It was 11.00am when two of their early lectures had finished and they walked the short distance to the Half Moon to meet with Stuie, who had surpassed himself by rising in time to be there. It did not go unnoticed and comments were passed. Squeezing out another of those suppressed laughs between closed teeth, Stuie explained, 'Well actually I can't claim all the credit. It was the cleaner that woke me!'

Before long they realised that lunchtime had come and gone and they were more than a bit tipsy, not to mention foolish to have relied on a liquid lunch. The fresh air hit them square in the face as they stepped out onto the pavement and made their way precariously across the road, feeling their way past the hotel on uneven paving before turning sharp left at the next junction. What happened shortly after that was a blur for most, but it entailed them walking on the road – which they thought was safer and less uneven – a discourteous driver of middling years and two of them sporting rugby shorts, light T-shirts and sandals, as they had become accustomed to wearing. While one chose the pavement to show their discontent with the driver, another pushed up against the driver-side window, so that the driver was left in no doubt as to whom the gesture was meant for.

They took off at speed and made their escape across the footbridge where no car could follow, panting heavily from the exertion which running now presented. Collapsing onto their respective beds, they crawled under a bedspread and were fast asleep within seconds. It had just turned midday.

They made it for tea, which would be their only meal that day. They devoured extra portions of the all-day breakfast by getting on the right side of the servers: always a priority task, especially with an influx of new staff to continue the tradition. After all, they were growing boys. Or at least that was their excuse, which female staff especially always seemed to accept readily and without question.

Making the most of teatime, they paid visits to their growing friend base to invite them out for evening entertainment and to celebrate. 'We're meeting up at the Travellers Rest first at about 8pm.' Stuie shared this with two first years, Ali and Cathy, who lived in Ravensworth Terrace, immediately renamed Ravens Perch the following day to register its significance in the Stooges' lives.

Due to excesses earlier in the day, the evening was quite controlled in terms of alcohol intake. It made a welcome change to see things and people clearly and avoid embarrassing conversations the following day. They ended up at a night venue and danced the night away and in their own way. Stuie's were understated movements, with barely a voluntary sway to maximise his conversation time with whoever was opposite him. Leo's were more adventurous and likely to send those closest to him running for cover or another drink. The music mattered not to him it seemed, as his arms alternately flailed and then dropped in loops, ending up under his armpits or behind him out of sight. The eye contact between the three of them accentuated particularly at the sight of one of them netting a beautiful catch.

So it was that night that George's reward for his special day was to dance with a girl he had admired from afar since the first term of that second year, but thought was entirely out of his league. His movements were more muted than Leo's, but reasonably flamboyant to be recognisable from a distance and varied in nature. Stuie had managed to secure Ali towards the end of the evening, while George spent a large part of the evening with Cathy, whose shoulder length blond hair mesmerised him as it turned from side to side with her head movements and bounced in time with her ample breasts, drawing dangerously close to him on more than one occasion.

'How are you enjoying your birthday?' she asked, as the evening was drawing to a close. Thinking more clearly than he had ever done before, he ventured 'It's been good, but would be even better if you would be my girlfriend.' She gasped, a little surprised at his frankness, but the broad smile and engaging muffled laugh that followed told him that his boldness was about to pay off.

'Of course I would,' she responded wholeheartedly with anticipation, 'I'd be delighted.'

'Marvellous!' came the stunned reaction, 'Shall we go?'

The walk back along the towpath could not have been more romantic, with a near full moon in evidence on a clear night. They sauntered arm in arm on their own. The others had left a little before them and the stillness of the river in the small hours absorbed them. He walked her home, planted a kiss tenderly on her lusciously soft lips and said good night.

Returning to relate the amazing culmination of a term and a half's longing, George shared his excitement with the other two, who were delighted at his good fortune.

Stuie had to admit 'I had a great time with Ali. She's really funny but don't think it's going anywhere romantically, as I got the brush off at the end… in the nicest possible way though.' Leo's night had been drawn more to the beer and he had split at an earlier stage, not seeing anyone likely to give him the eye in the closing songs.

'How did you do it?' questioned Leo. 'Don't know. Just lucky I guess. Having a birthday helped and…' George went on thoughtfully, 'I suppose I have to thank Flaubert a little for his insights into the hitherto unknown female psyche.'

'Oooh Madame Bovary! So the reading list from last year did have a purpose then after all?' Leo's revelation was purely rhetorical. 'I'll have to reread that and properly this time!'

The passing days saw George riding on a cushion of air, judging by his unusually bouncy gait even in those sandals, striped blue T-shirt and beret. Alas, this habitual way of dressing for both George and Leo landed them both in hotter water than they had anticipated or wished for. They were summoned into the administrative office to be handed an official-looking, signed-for envelope each. They both sat down heavily in the JCR armchairs with disbelief and a heavy heart. They had both been identified and reported to the police for indecent exposure during their cavorting around on their return from the pub that morning.

Stuie was sympathetic but could not conceal his mirth at the others' situation and his own incredible good fortune, not to say relief, at not having taken part in said actions.

There was nowhere to run or hide from the justice shortly to be meted out to them and they had their day in court and were both bound over to keep the peace for three years. It was sobering enough to change their attitude to overindulgence which, though it happened less regularly, was always there in the background. Indeed on one memorable occasion, they found themselves asleep in the wee small hours on tarmac, three abreast lying flat on their backs in the middle of a road, albeit a quiet road. They contemplated at length the University cricket first team – for no other reason than the pitch lay immediately below and in front of them – and how the composition of the team were mostly from their college. They moved onto the stars, once sitting up was no longer possible or desirable. Waking at around 3am, when the cold began to permeate their fairly thin clothing layer, they leaned on one elbow to see to their left the unmistakeable and imposing high wall with what appeared to be a huge rounded growth on top. So unnatural it was, seeming to extend in the same way on the other side. This made it unscalable from both sides and, equally incongruously, stood side by side with semi-detached, red brick housing in that part of the city. The sight of Her Majesty's Prison shook them to the core. The sobering up was swift and remained with them all the way down the winding road, which took them to the pitch and across the river, before falling gratefully into their welcoming beds.

Planning Ahead

The rest of that academic year was spent indulging in university and city life to the full.

The French set were all making preparations for their year abroad. Out of a set of sixty, all bar six of their number were found academic institutions to go to, in exchange for a commitment to attend lectures or classes in French and they were to be billeted in university accommodation abroad. This certainly did not appeal to Leo and George who, having taken a gap year out, did not see the value in continuing within academic walls, when there was a great big world out there waiting for them. Just as well, because they were among the six who were not found positions and so had to fend for themselves, with little or no help from the university. 'Great.' was George's initial reaction followed by a rhetorical, 'What are we paying for again?'

'Yeah, that sucks alright.' replied Leo, 'Have to pull a few strings at home I guess to see what they can come up with.' No such luck or connections for George, for whom this became a major concern. Where to work? Where to live? Above all… where to start!

Racking his brain during some enforced down time on the college lawns, his mind began to race 'I know nothing about industries or business in France. No doubt they have a different vocabulary for each business sector which I won't know. Just like the nautical specialised vocabulary in English. I've no experience of dealing with French companies. What can I do based on my previous experience … go and pump fuel in a filling station or pack electronics parts? That doesn't sound like much fun. Oh hell, what am I going to do?' Another fear loomed large – the fear of failure!

As no one was in the immediate vicinity, he didn't expect a reply, but wished for all he was worth that a sign or flash of inspiration would come tumbling out of the cherry tree he found himself under. Just then several blossoms were lifted by a gentle breeze which came and went, separating them from their anchorages and floated gently down in front of him, into his hair and onto his nose.

The sign *ville fleurie* came back to him from a former trip travelling through the French countryside on his way down to Normandy. Pulling up hard at a set of small rounded, pedestrian-level traffic lights, the coach paused on the edge of a town, the name of which was long forgotten. What was not, were those two words *ville fleurie* written as a declaration of intent above a beautiful raised border, encased in railway sleepers, the rich earth brimming with petunias, cascading lobelia and French marigolds naturally. His memory scanned beneath that splendour to encounter three more words: *ville jumelée avec* … followed by three or four international town names in Germany, Holland and England.

Even with his limited knowledge, he remembered *jumeaux* meant twins and he recalled that his nearest home town had such a twinning arrangement. A flicker of light ignited at that moment, which raised his spirits and gave him a purpose: a mini-research project, which was just what he was looking for.

Of course he knew no one there, but one of the takeaway quotes from French lessons at school had been,

> Don't underestimate the power of the mayor in any town in France.

So he wrote a letter to the mayor explaining his predicament and asked him for help. His reply implied that he would ask companies in the area to reach out directly to George. 'Not quite what I was expecting, but it's a step in the right direction.' thought George to himself, 'Now it's a waiting game.'

Now that things were out of his control for the time being, he allowed himself the luxury of soaking up the sunshine on the lawns and going to croquet parties at distant colleges up the hill to get to know more of the French set members personally. They collectively realised that not only were they about to embark on their year abroad, but also the only people they would know on their return would be their set. Not only that, but as many would find out, they could meet up while over there to support each other in what would otherwise turn out to be a stultifyingly boring existence in an extended, vaguely dystopian academia, frustrated by an absence of 'difference' from what had gone before. The experience anticipated was a cultural change for sure, but the restrictions placed on them by their academic hosts merely served to institutionalise their life.

Other distractions to be savoured were: long evening conversations into the night; walks back by the river breathing in the soporific scent of wild garlic growing on the steep banks under beech and sycamore trees; attending an evening performance of Midsummer Night's Dream by an old ruin well into the night and staying up, as the group of six did on more than one occasion, to witness the dawn of a new day.

Planning Ahead

Playing sport was more leisurely in the summer, with tennis featuring large and cheering on the college rowing team, as they competed in the Head of the River races. One advantage of being invited into this university college, as a former Physical Education teacher training college, was the exhaustive schedule of sports fixtures with teams from outside the university in local leagues. The college supplied almost all of the 1st XI cricket team and large swathes of rugby players, some of whom were destined for the varsity colleges to facilitate a smooth path to an international career.

Also there to enjoy, at least for George, was the company of Cathy. Additionally, new American friends had arrived from Penn State University and one was attached very much to Ali, while another – the insuppressible Bunny – became firm friends with George's group, as well as most other people she met. But for George, Cathy stood out head and shoulders above the rest – from the way her nose wrinkled up when she laughed, her generous smile heightened by full cheeks, to her strawberry blond hair parted down the middle sweeping off to both sides of her face and her magnificent figure and the ladylike way she sat with knees to the side as if she were riding side-saddle. He adored her.

Where Cathy was buoyant but reserved, Ali was flamboyant. Her very curly, black tresses graced a lily-white neck in open topped blouses, pinched in on her tiny waist. Her preference was for light, flowing fairy-like skirts, layered to conceal stately legs but effectively highlighting a generous figure above the waist. She was indeed magical.

Even though the term's end was only a few days away, George, Leo and Stuie were still in full summer swing, soaking up the warming rays under almost cloudless days and immersing themselves in the ambiance of warm evenings in great company. It was at one such social evening – unbeknown to them that it would be their last – where laughter, drink and dancing were in harmony. They broke up in the early hours, with George and Cathy taking the road leading down to the cricket square, pausing at a knee-high brick perimeter wall.

'I think we should stop now while we're ahead. What with me going into my final year, I'm going to have my hands full and what, with you going abroad…'

The words fell like an axe through George's empty skull. Cathy kept on talking; George's stupefied expression concealed a torrent of emotions, swirling about in a void. He could not look at Cathy, staring into space and barely managing an 'I see'.

Moose Conquering Fear

Cathy's words tapered off into indistinct mumblings and nervous pained contortions, which replaced that hitherto ever-present smile. 'This cannot be happening,' he barely suppressed his thoughts, almost doubled up in this worst of fears, 'not now and not to me.'

One foot after another, a memory returned from the past three or four months, punctuated with a knot in his stomach at what was once and is now gone. 'Chalk it down to experience.' he imagined the irrelevant, misunderstanding friendly advice would be when he got back. The only word which echoed the truth was 'down'. He had thought only recently – even taking a little pride in his achievement – how far he had come in this relationship stuff but now, it seemed, building up hopes was a futile affair, leaving expectations dashed to oblivion. She had planned ahead for this and he had not.

Off to France

The rest of that summer was muted for George. The absence of work for the year abroad, however, helped focus a small percentage of his mind on that task, but with little impact on his thoughts, which continued to dog him well into his first few months in France.

As it happened, two companies came forward generously to offer work to him. One had sent him a postcard of a four-star restaurant with a thatched roof growing over small windows like hooded eyebrows, with larger French windows at ground level. The menu was certainly enticing, but the location was out of town, so transport would be necessary.

The second was a brief business invitation letter to be a *stagiaire* for one year, with a broad letterhead proclaiming their brand name *Cuivre et Alliages*. Knowing precious little about metals linked with copper, he was intrigued to find out more. It seemed like his options were simple: a placement in an industry or become a waiter in a high-class restaurant.

'Well I know where I'm going to learn more French.' he said jokingly, as he talked it through with his parents.

'But where will you stay?' came the naturally concerned maternal instinct.

'Oh, I haven't worked that out yet. I suppose I will sort it out once there.'

'You can't do that. Try to sort it out before then.' they both replied in unison.

'We can take you over with us this summer if you like.' came the ever generous and welcome suggestion from his sister. 'We're going over to France the second week of August and I'm sure we can take a little detour.'

'Oh that's fantastic sis.' George said, giving her a loving hug for being there for him… again.

What looked like a little detour on the map turned out to be a five hour round trip from their planned location to the middle of Burgundy. The car echoed to the sound of his apologies.

'Seems like they used to be great friends of the English kings many centuries ago, so I hope they'll still be welcoming!' George wondered out loud, as he stepped down from the car and made his way to the tourist information bureau in the market square.

They were indeed very welcoming and after a few phone calls, came back to report that it was their busy period at that moment and all accommodation was fully booked. He felt extremely guilty when relating the failure of the mission and apologised to his sister and boyfriend again for their wasted time. 'Don't be silly. It was worth a go' they comforted, 'and at least you can check out some local landmarks, including your future workplace.'

The industrial estate lay just outside the town and only two or three kilometres away from the centre, which was eminently walkable. 'That's a relief.' sighed George.

With that they headed back, spending a few days en route taking in Paris and making a few stops on the way.

'No need to unpack much, as you'll be setting off again in another couple of weeks.' ribbed his father. Exciting though this was, there was still a twinge of guilt, mixed in with a hint of nervous trepidation, not to mention the residual sinking feeling in his stomach of facing it alone without the reassurance of a love waiting back in England. He missed her still.

Before he knew it, George was sat on a train with everything he thought he needed for spending nearly a whole year away, packed into two large, bulging suitcases. One older black case with a leather double handle and substantial chunky metal zips and a slightly newer brown one, whose flimsier plastic zips were straining to contain his clothes.

He lugged them from platform to platform, as several changes were necessary before stepping onto the newly introduced TGV heading round Paris and down to Dijon.

He stepped out thankfully into the late morning sunshine in Dijon, taking in the beautiful floral displays, conveniently placed to make commuting more tolerable he thought. He headed to a taxi rank before completing his journey, arriving back at the market square where he had been only two weeks previously.

Off to France

He did not recognise the staff at the information bureau, so had to reintroduce his purpose for being there and his burning request for accommodation. He did however recognise the same response that came back only too quickly.

Vous pouvez revenir dans deux heures et on verra s'il y a quelque chose de nouveau.

The situation wasn't much better than last time, with the exception that a small hotel had just the one room available for that night, for one night only. Deciding to take it one day, or now one hour at a time, they booked it by phone for him.

Wondering what to do in the meantime, he decided to make his way out to the factory as he knew his way there. Here there were two major differences between last time and this. Previously it had been overcast whereas now the sun was at its height. Before, he had been given a lift by his sister. Now he had to walk the two kilometres on foot with a heavy suitcase in each hand.

One of George's tenets had been to always finish what you start. He no doubt considered it a strength, others more likely a stubbornness, bordering on insanity. To him, this was his mission that day.

Arriving out of breath at the entrance which remained open, he staggered to a small side entrance of the long orange factory building and bumped into a man in blue overalls making his hasty exit.

Excusing himself in less than adequate French, he asked to see M. Poissonet and was shown to an office of meagre proportions and quite spartan with it. 'Functional', he thought, 'That's practical. I can live with that.' Smiling at the managing director, he introduced himself in his best schoolboy French. 'What were the last two years at university about? When push comes to shove, you have to fall back onto the familiar phrases from school!'

The gentleman spoke at length, which George caught most of and he understood his last request for any questions. 'Well,' he said in poor French – as he struggled to find the word for salary and failed – then ventured apologetically 'how much will you pay me?'

'Mon Dieu...' he began, 'Pay you? *Non, non, non. C'est l'université qui vous paie! C'est l'université*', he repeated for the hard of French hearing.

There was no need for the repetition. He felt affronted and something stirred inside him, which had done so years earlier when he felt compelled to reprimand a rowdy set of French children in their tent, during his stint as a *moniteur* at the age of fifteen. He lost all inhibitions about the words that came out and said firmly in broken French, 'Marvellous. I have been unemployed before, but never in a foreign country with nowhere to live.' He could see himself back on that same train by evening!

He turned and left his office without so much as a glance back, picked up his bags and stormed out awkwardly through the side door, back towards the town centre.

He had only gone a few yards along the pavement, when one case – the black one, the more substantial one – dropped to the ground. Glancing down, he could not believe his eyes and implored the Almighty. 'Oh my God, what else could possibly go wrong?'

The handle had come away at one end, giving him no option but to lift it up onto one shoulder and steady it with one hand, while holding the other case in the other hand. 'I don't bloody-well believe it!' issued several times from his lips as he fought back the tears that began to force their way through. George rested a few times on the way back and was resolved that this would be his first and last day in France.

So distressed was George, that the staff at the information bureau showed their resourcefulness, as one of them remembered there was one Englishman that lived in the town. They would ring him to see what could be done. They restated, as before, that there was regrettably still no accommodation available. 'Why would there be,' he pondered dejectedly, 'they're probably still on vacation as schools don't go back for another week.'

Tom, the Englishman, came on the phone and explained in severely broken English that he could not come today, but would meet with George the following morning at the bureau. 'Go and get some sleep' was his advice.

'Sleep? Ha, fat chance of that!' George scoffed, after he had put the phone down.

There was nothing for it but to trek another kilometre or so to the small hotel, which could put him up for one night. By this time it was nine in the evening when, exhausted, he pushed the bell which brought someone to the frosted glass door. All he could make out through the dimly lit aluminium-surround door was a diminutive male figure, who opened it and greeted him warmly. '*Bonsoir monsieur. Mais qu'est-ce qui vous est arrivé... un petit accident?*' His glance down at the broken handle told George what his tired brain was at pains to translate. *'Ah oui'* he managed to squeeze out, with a small shrug of the shoulders.

With their world-renowned explanatory gestures, no doubt dating back centuries after more centuries of trying to explain themselves to foreigners like George, the concierge added *'Je m'en occuperai. Vous en faites pas. Vous videz la valise and laissez-la avec moi. D'accord?'*

The raised tone at the end of the sentence George recognised as requiring a response, even though the only words he caught were *vider* to empty, *valise* suitcase, and *laisser* leave. He tried to construct a *bona fide* future tense with *vider* but fell back on *aller* to say he was going to empty, without saying what he was emptying. He was led to the top of a stairwell, pushed open the door and both suitcases dropped to the floor of their own accord. He was whacked. Stirring himself and resisting all temptations to crash on the bed – which he knew would be fatal – he took all his things out of the broken suitcase and left it outside the door as requested. After which he flopped too tired to be emotional about anything. 'Tomorrow's another day…' he thought before losing consciousness.

Another Day

When he came to, a few rays slipped through the partially open curtain from the night before, which at the time was definitely a low priority. His arms ached, his legs complained at what they'd been put through the previous day, but he pushed up on one arm to scan his room in daylight. Not four or even three-star, but it was clean, neat and tidy with a pleasant décor. He would not have chosen orange but that didn't matter. He was rested. As his eyes moved towards the door, there just to the left of it, lay his black suitcase open and with the handle back in place.

He leapt out of bed to try the handle – firm as anything – 'What an amazing job!' he exclaimed out loud. Dashing through his customary morning ablutions, he raced downstairs to be greeted by the same fellow as the night before. The concierge began with an apology. 'What? No,' George protested in week phrases, 'what is this?' but he insisted. He had tracked down a friend, who was most apologetic because he had no new rivets to reattach the handle with, so he had had to use old ones!

Remembering that this was well after 9pm, George wondered what wonderful place he had come to and how blessed he had been to have stayed under this man's roof. He would not forget this act of kindness for as long as he lived, he asserted, confining himself to say simply 'I will not forget this' to his host. Those same rivets were still in place twelve years later and, indeed, outlived the rest of the case.

After a complimentary croissant and bowl of coffee, George set off back to the tourist information bureau to wait on Tom's arrival. He was looking up at the campanile on the square, when a faded, dark blue, practical car drew up alongside him. Out stepped what was an unmistakeably English gentleman in all his incongruous eccentricity. His black-grey coiffure was erratic, with a quiff at the front and supported by a generous but crooked smile, as he felt for his now unfamiliar mother tongue.

'Sorry to be late ol' chap.' Tom began as though he was quoting from Sherlock Holmes, or some other quintessentially English novel. 'Shall we try to sort out your situation? Come along. Follow me.' and they entered the bureau. The friendly greeting of the staff to Tom reassured George that he was in good hands, and assured Tom of using their phone to arrange to see the mayor.

Another Day

'Oh, so you know the mayor?' George asked. 'That's useful, as it was him who proposed the work placements for me.'

'Sure,' said Tom confidently, 'we go back a long way. I've been in France seventeen years, the last eleven here in Nuits. We've had our run-ins but he's always invited to my tastings and hosts the annual St. Vincent festival.' Before he had a chance to ask, Tom filled George in on his life, aspirations, the annual events of the region and how he hoped to be inducted into the *Confrérie des Chevaliers du Tastevin*, whose meeting place and base was in what was, and still is, one of the most famous vineyards in Burgundy: Clos Vougeot. Here began George's education into viticulture and wine tasting, which it turned out was Tom's profession. Tom added, 'Founded by the Cistercian monks. They built the wall around it and came from Citeaux, a local monastery that makes some phenomenal cheese.' He was not wrong, as George would shortly testify to at dinner that evening. George mused out loud 'Monks always chose the best locations, it seems to me, and now it seems that they really knew the pick of locations for the best wine.' On this they could both agree. Tom had grown up in Yorkshire and was familiar with many of the ruined abbeys there.

Their short walk to the *mairie* was at an end and George felt butterflies in his stomach, as they entered the impressive building with huge, crossed French flags adorning the entrance.

Arriving in the mayor's office, Tom explained the situation much more succinctly in French and even before he had finished, the mayor was already holding the telephone to his ear waiting for the dial tone to end. The tirade in French which ensued went way over George's head. If the mayor's expression was anything to go by, then the *président–directeur–général* or PDG for short was getting a right mayoral chewing out… or so he hoped.

'I think we should now pay the director a visit. Hop in and let's see what he has to say for himself.' George didn't dare ask any more, so as not to jinx the situation. Tom dropped him outside the factory and waited in the car park. Pushing open the director's office door, George avoided his gaze to start with, but the more conciliatory tone made him look up in time to see the hint of a faint smile, before he bade him goodbye with a brief *à lundi*.

'Wow. It's true what they say, "what a difference a day makes".' George muttered to himself, while crossing the car park.

Moose Conquering Fear

He thanked Tom profusely for his intervention and his relief was palpable. 'You must come and eat with us tonight. Marie, my wife, would love to meet you,' Tom offered kindly, 'but first, let's see if any accommodation has come up.' Great though this dramatic turn of events on the work front had been, it was only half the story. George sat down opposite the lady in the bureau dreading the worst.

'Well,' she said, 'you're in luck, as something just came to us only an hour ago. Here's the address if you'd like to take a look at it.'

'At this point, I'll take anything.' he thought when, just twenty-four hours ago, he had nothing but a return journey to contemplate. As he settled back into Tom's car seat, after a successful visit and meeting a lovely landlady – whose daughter worked at the factory too – a tear squeezed out of one eye as the realisation overcame him. 'Someone is looking down on me today…' he sighed with relief.

Life in Burgundy

Settling down in Nuits-St-Georges was made relatively easy by a painstakingly attentive landlady, who had thought of everything. The ground floor flat was self-sufficient with its own covered walkway to a door, cunningly concealed under their upper floor and adjacent balcony, but in no way was it overlooked. Very private, with a mixture of mature planting which attracted birds and butterflies in equal numbers. An easy on the ear, tinkling bell announced any visitors to the house at the wrought iron gate, through which anyone new would look and think they had arrived at the entrance to a tropical paradise. Such a myriad of large and small shiny dark green leaves greeted the eye, some with cut outs others more fern-like in appearance, all overlapping with each other. Some were as high as the top of the roof, but from the road you could still make out a splendour of geraniums boasting pinks and reds, spilling over in a nonordered manner the length of the balcony above: a balcony with two slender wooden rails above a small walled parapet, which provided the backdrop to the more upright geraniums. A white classic Citroen nestled beneath the big leaves, guarded by a massive brut of a dog with a big heart – almost certainly a mix containing St. Bernard in his genes somewhere. No corner of the courtyard had been wasted and much was reused: for example, a small polypin-sized cask had had its side – including its black metal retaining rings – partially removed, set on its side with the tap still in situ, ready for some fresh planting. Hanging as it did from a triangular metal hook on one of the square, vertical, stone columns, George was captivated by it at first sight!

From his threshold in the shade, George stepped down onto light brown flagstones which he expected to be cold but were in fact warm – as if warmed by the sun during the day – which did not seem feasible to his logical mind. A dresser to the left housed all the French crockery, breakfast bowl, cutlery and cooking utensils he would need, together with other strangely shaped objects, whose use he had yet to fathom out. The bedroom, also to the left, looked out onto a small secluded courtyard with an exotically blossomed tree at its centre. There was no visible entrance onto it that he could see, but the sun's rays streamed delightfully through the windows, striping the bedspread in their comforting glow, which made him put his hand down on them to feel their warmth. He was not disappointed.

'This will do just fine', he mused to himself, 'I am so lucky that this became available when it did. Thank goodness for small mercies.'

Unpacking his two large suitcases was not taxing and it wasn't long before he was to have the best night's sleep ever.

Over the initial three months, his French was passable but poor. Rookie mistakes were in abundance and misunderstandings a daily occurrence and an obstacle to progress. But then there was the *pâtisserie* lady, who was always kind enough to correct his grammar and syntax mistakes, as well as providing him with the most magnificent *millefeuilles* to die for. Her *vitrine* ran almost half the length of one side of a triangular *place* – it seems incoherent to call it a square when it was that shape – always spotlessly clean, a dazzling display with multi-coloured delicacies to tempt all passers-by. None were spared their magnificence and the smell of newly baked baguettes coming from the other half of her premises pulled you in like a tractor beam. She was irrepressible in her smiling countenance and good humour, in spite of rising every day at 4am with her husband to start the baking and cooking cycle. Quite remarkable dedication to making people's lives so much richer for knowing them and kinder too for the kindnesses they bestowed on their clientele, making them feel very much welcome on every occasion.

Almost directly opposite the rear of her shop lived one of the *polisseuses*, a lady from the factory, who was particularly tickled by his announcement one day in conversation with the three women who worked the polishing machine. George was keen to let them know that transport was not a problem for him, as he was now the proud owner of a red Volkswagen Beetle or *coccinelle* as they would say.

Trying to be cool about it and wanting to translate a popular phrase into French – never a good idea, especially when this one was in fact of American origin, even worse idea – he blurted out loudly, '*Pas de problème. J'ai des roues maintenant!*' General outpouring of mirth all round, as Babette fell about laughing and the others tried to clarify, '*Tes roues? T'as des roues, toi?*'

He couldn't tell if the word was badly chosen, badly pronounced or totally inappropriate, perhaps with sexual connotations which he was unfamiliar with. 'Oh well, at least it made them laugh,' he thought, but like a running joke it came back to haunt him on a weekly basis. They were not about to let him escape so easily. The more it went on, the more he assumed his pronunciation was at fault, so he worked on it more.

He was indebted however to Babette, as it was she who remarked on his staple diet after the first three weeks and rightly assumed that he could make nothing else to eat.

His *casse-croûte* consisted of a baguette bought that day, a weekly supply of pâté or smashed pork from the only charcuterie he found en route to the factory and tomatoes. After the first two months he was tempted to add a bottle of red burgundy to the fridge, which enhanced it immensely and seemed to be acceptable to many working there.

It was Babette who kindly offered to show him the way to make a genuine French dressing with Dijon white wine mustard, wine vinegar and sunflower oil. He dropped into her house at the end of a day and after his short instruction, they repaired to a café nearby for a quick *apéro'* before supper. More instruction followed, as she made him aware of some local customs including the ordering of a *canon*, which reminded him of the rocket fuel label he had previously encountered behind the college bar. They shared similar explosive qualities, since the *canon* was short for *canon de rouge*, referring to a small glass of local, red burgundy.

This led to an extended conversation about the wine people brought into work for lunch. The most cost-effective way, she explained in French, was to order a *cubitinaire* – a plastic cubic container about as tall as his knee – from a local *cave*. 'You are pretty much guaranteed to be drinking good burgundy, no matter which brand you choose' she confided. This George decided to do the same weekend, while it was still fresh in his mind, which was becoming increasingly fuzzy he had to admit. At the same time he thought the proprietor of the café might have closed the blinds, but a glance at the *terrasse* outside confirmed that it was already dark!

'Well I must be going.' he excused himself in passable French this time. 'Maybe it was true,' he thought, 'that drink helps you speak a language more fluently… up to the point where you can no longer stand upright of course.'

The cooling summer breeze passed pleasantly over his face as he made his way back to his accommodation. '*Neuf heures, ben Dieu'*, he exclaimed, while feeling for the gate latch and congratulating himself on his growing acclimatisation to the French vernacular.

'That's the first time I've missed dinner… or rather replaced it with a night on *pastis'*, he mused, skipping all his usual preparations for bed before collapsing onto it, fully clothed.

The morning rays beamed at him from the internal courtyard and forced him to rise, as did the temperature too. 'Ah yes, the *cubitinaire*!' he enthused, surprised at his own short memory recall for once. Luckily for him the nearest *Viticulteur, propriétaire récoltant* was a little way down the riverside road. River was a rather exaggerated name for the Meuzin, encased as it was in an expansive twenty metre-wide and six metre-deep concrete shell traversing the town, presumably in case torrential rains poured down off the gentle Côte d'Or slopes towering above it, all of two hundred metres high at most. Decades of disuse had coated some of the base in a faded green growth, barely surviving the lack of water which for the most part was reduced to a trickle down the V-shape cut into the middle of this shell.

It was a pleasant walk though as he skipped on and off the pavement between pollarded lime trees which lined the river walk, to escape the vehicles parked unceremoniously, covering half the pedestrian's right of way. His understanding of unintelligible road signs improved, when he noticed how all of the same cars religiously jumped across onto the opposite side of the road about half way through each month.

Choosing what would elsewhere be considered an ordinary table wine, George knew from his chat the previous evening, that any *pinot noir* Bourgogne would knock spots off those found back in England and surpass even those found in other wine regions in France. The advice he'd received was spot on. After a brief *dégustation*, he put the large *cubi*, as it was known, onto his shoulder and carried it the short distance home. A warm feeling came over him as he realised after two months of living abroad, that he had come not just to accept this location, but preferred it to his other home. That village now seemed a very long way away. So much had happened, so much resolved and so much learnt and still to learn. His co-workers and now friends at the factory had played a large part in that.

Life on the Factory Floor

The acrid stench of anodising chemicals at one end of the factory was where George was sent to work under Marcel, a huge frame of a man with a medium-length, grey beard, black-rimmed spectacles and a welcoming smile. Making sure the aluminium profiles were attached by small clamps to the vertical dipping bars was his first task, using protective gloves. The glow and heat from the press at the other end of the open plan factory floor could be felt the length of the building. Some employees he felt sure ambled frequently in that direction, especially during the first two winter months, to benefit from the hot aluminium profiles, which emanated slowly but surely from the cast iron press.

As he walked past the searing heat, he noticed a manufacturer's plate, which to his amazement bore the place name Manchester in a font and size that reminded him of steam traction engines: emblazoned with unmistakeably proud and chunky gold lettering, like Burrell and Fowler & Sons. It swiftly took him back to the smoky stacks belching out black coal clouds, yet immaculately turned out red and green liveries with gleaming brass governors spinning round, as they chug-chugged their way past his house, on their way to a field by the recreation ground for their annual steam engine rally. They came from miles around to show off their ploughing skills – those were predominantly the black Fowler engines – or to let the kids climb up onto the steps, to be shown the controls and of course pull on the whistle, before jumping down from what seemed like an enormous height.

His daydream was shaken by a firm hand grasping his arm as he was introduced to Dédé, the profile quality control engineer, who remarked, 'Made in Manchester, you'll have noticed?' in perfectly passable English.

'Yes I did. It seems quite old to still be going.' George remarked and continued, 'Quite unexpected, but at the same time comforting, to have a familiar name from the home country, pushing out such welcome warmth.'

'Come with me,' said Dédé, 'I want to show you something.' With that he ushered George into a room almost opposite the hottest part of the press, but once inside with the door shut, it was the quietest room he had come across to date.

On the floor were several round but large iron casts, much like the multiple tap and die sets, which his father had shown him how to use to make screws and nuts. This was very similar to the thread die he recalled, only much larger and much, much heavier.

Dédé sat down to use an air line on the one nearest to him. He explained how every piece of dust and dirt must not find its way into that profile, as it would result in an entire fifty metre length of aluminium bar being ruined, with a scratch running along its length.

'What are these bars used for?' asked George, curious about the end product now, having witnessed anodisation, polishing and plain finishes. 'Most will be surrounds for windows, patio doors and retail shop windows, shipping out to destinations in France, to former colonies in Africa and other parts of Europe.'

'This old girl may be old,' Dédé went on referring to the press, 'but she's lasted way beyond her projected life… and what's more, she was only supposed to be operated eight hours a day. Here she has been operating 24 hours a day across three shifts, as you know.'

'Incredible,' said George in awe, 'I'm on earlies and lates at the moment, but expect to be put on nights soon.'

He thanked Dédé and walked back to a Marcel, who looked perplexed as to where his newest recruit had got to, but was tolerant enough when he heard what he had learnt. Marcel shared with him that he was also a *vigneron* and that this was his second job, to supplement what he hoped one day would sell as a *grand cru*. George had heard the same desire from Tom's lips too, but Tom was an *'émigré* from the UK, albeit seventeen years ago. He had come down from Paris to follow his dream, whereas Marcel was a local, born and bred in Corgoloin. Their passion, however, for Burgundian wines was identical.

George was not looking forward to night shifts as it brought back memories of his own father, who had been largely absent from his youth, due to shift work. He also remembered the change which working middle shifts brought about, after sitting Craftsman Engineer exams in his mid-50s, a feat which was both remarkable and humbling for them both. He had to go back to school essentially and had turned to George to help him, as George was in the sixth form at the time taking Pure and Applied Maths as two of his A levels.

Working from that related experience, he hoped for the same for himself at some point during the year. As it was, he didn't have to wait long.

Life on the Factory Floor

The middle part of the building was run by Alain, who had an Italian sounding surname and his dark, short hair gave credence to the claim. He had no idea to begin with, but Alain certainly played to his audience to make the most of the connection, however tenuous it was. He was in his early 40s and fairly short – but then most were shorter than George, who was to be christened by Alain with the nickname of *gran'baccala*, owing to that fish's exceptional length. Only much later would he understand that this salted codfish is seen as a particular favourite by Italians everywhere. Above all, Alain had a tremendous, playful sense of humour to get him and his workforce through the day. It was clear from his direction and brisk walking between different sections, that he was the manager of the floor once the aluminium profiles had cooled down and had been cut into lengths for processing as per the customer orders.

He wasted no time, having talked to George on one or two occasions during his second month, in inviting him into the offices, for the first time since that disastrous meeting with the Managing Director, or PDG (*Président–Directeur–Général*) as Alain and others called him. George had the pejorative connotation quickly explained to him under muted breath.

'*Venez*. Come in', he motioned to George, ushering him in, 'We have a test for you to take. Are you up for it?'

'Sure, what's at stake?' pushed George.

'Oh, just an aptitude test.' Alain explained more, 'You see that box over by the wall? Make yourself comfortable and guide the electrode around the shape without touching the edges.'

'Crazy', thought George, taken back once again to the fairground attractions accompanying the annual steam rallies that had taken place in his village. Reminiscing to himself, he recalled 'This is exactly like the game where we won money for moving a similar electrode hoop along a wire, bent into loops and contortions along its length. That was child's play and the winnings much appreciated, when he handed them over to his mum.'

'Ok,' he confirmed to Alain, 'I'll give it my best shot.' In less than ten seconds he had passed around the simple contour of a question mark shape and put the hoop down.

'I knew you'd have no bother.' declared Alain and, on leaving the office, added 'So now you can drive the overhead crane. Do you fancy that?'

Moose Conquering Fear

'For real?' said a stupefied George thinking to himself, 'You mean I can now drive a bridge crane above all these workers, with loads of up to a maximum of one metric tonne – as he had learnt from Alain earlier – based on that simple test?' This had to be unreal. But no, it wasn't. There was more 'Of course you'll have to work middle shifts now, you realise. Will that work for you?'

'You bet,' replied George in the affirmative most confidently, though with a little trepidation. 'Don't worry,' Alain assured him, 'I'll show you all you need to know. Let's go and see Marcel now.'

Oh hell, yes. In all his excitement he had forgotten that he'd be letting Marcel down after the briefest of apprenticeships, but he thanked him profusely for the experience and Marcel was completely understanding. 'I thought I might not have you for long, but you must come over to lunch on Saturday to meet Paul and Agnès. It's Paul's 18th – we can show you how we celebrate birthdays Burgundy-style.' Intriguing, he thought.

So it was all arranged at the drop of a hat. Shift changes made, lunch booked, more experiences to savour with no doubt some excellent wine to boot. 'Onwards and upwards', he mused, as the spring in his step returned.

A birthday like no other

Saturday came round quickly and the delayed rise till after the sun was up meant more sleep to prepare for the event. 'Just bring yourself. Come on over to our house at, say eleven o'clock' had been Marcel's parting words to him, before he left for the day.

Driving south down the now familiar D974 in the direction of Beaune, he passed the unprepossessing quarries at Comblanchien, with their huge yellow-orange blocks hewn from the hillside, impressive for their size but not for the damage to the Côte that came with it.

George pulled up in front of Marcel's house, where there was ample room on the roadside. A glance down the slope into what would normally be his garage, revealed a complete conversion into a fully laden set of trestle tables on three sides of a rectangle, with the open end facing up the drive. Already people were gathering at the tables, all standing and greeting one another. Into the fray George launched himself with what was becoming an easier language for him now.

He had always been warned that it may take up to three months to become almost fluent in the language. The first two stages had come and gone – catching all sounds, though not understanding everything and responding in kind were under his belt. He was now looking forward to approaching the third stage in the third month of his stay.

Paul and Agnès were quick to come over and introduce themselves. Paul's mop of longish, thick brown hair blew across his face, giving him a dishevelled look and he was by far the loudest voice there, perhaps by right as it was his birthday after all. As far as George could tell no one had yet been drinking, so that could not account for Paul's volume either. Agnès' hair was similar, though much more ordered in appearance: longer naturally, but still blessed with waves and curly volume down beyond her shoulders. She had a pleasant, slightly mischievous face, while Paul's was more serious with his eyes almost always concealed behind light orange sunglasses. The day had stayed bright for him. Marcel had much to be proud of in both of them.

It wasn't long before Marcel invited everyone to take their seats and the conversations and wine flowed in all quarters: a traditional *cass' blanc* – local *crème de cassis* and its partner of choice, the white a*ligoté* wine from the region.

Starters came and went, two in number, accompanied by a suitably light Burgundy from the Côte de Beaune. The main course was divided into separate platters for vegetables and meat, as was customary. The meat made its entrance with much fanfare by Marcel, who presented what appeared to be a jeroboam-sized wine bottle for all to partake of. Marcel explained how, on Paul's tenth birthday, he had purposely set aside several bottles of that year's vintage from his own vines, keeping them back for just this occasion. George knew from Tom that a good bottle of Nuits would be at its best after eight years, provided it was kept at the requisite 8-12°C for the duration. Marcel proudly lifted up the bottle for all to see with his own label on it, to rapturous applause from his audience.

George continued his conversation in depth with his neighbour and happened to glance up to find almost everyone had left the table.

'Where have they all gone to?' he enquired. Before his neighbour could answer they both felt the same need from their stomachs, which ordered them to stand and go for a walk. A glance at his watch surprised them both. It was 4pm already and with four courses down, helped on by two *digestifs* interspersed between courses, rising out of their chairs was considered nothing short of a miraculous achievement. To his astonishment, he felt neither light-headed nor overly full or bloated. So now he understood it when his colleagues would say with an inner confidence 'The French know how to eat' – the same equally could be said of Italians too of course as Alain was at pains to point out – they take their time, enjoy the good company and healthy discussion at table, eating beautifully prepared food in ample but measured quantities.

As they turned the corner at the side of the house, they set off away from the Chemin de Monsieur still feeling their stomachs, but by the time they had reached the corner of the Allée des Peupliers, their discomfort was already easing. To their collective hilarity, they encountered everyone else from the table doing exactly the same thing, but in the opposite direction. They had all taken a turn round the block before attempting the dessert courses.

Sat back in the garage once more, a colder *ratafia* – a *digestif* made by Marcel from the grape remnants which float on top of a vat, he explained, whereas *marc* is produced from the lees at the bottom – was put in front of them. This seemed to be some diabolic concoction of the two with added ingredients to delight the palate, while satiating any possible digestive problems. 'Should always be served cold', he reinforced. He was not wrong. It single-handedly eased his intestine to the point where he was not only able to take dessert, but was actively looking forward to it.

With a *poire Belle-Helène* placed before each of them, out came the champagne or rather, the *méthode champenoise* Burgundian equivalent, which far and away outstripped its more celebrated cousin from Champagne. This was reserved solely for the sweet dessert, while a return to a red burgundy was inevitable for the cheese course, crowned with a whole *rond* of Cîteaux: another monastical marvel, which had the knack of easing the palate for an altogether splendid closure to an amazing celebratory meal.

Je suis rassis. George pronounced, which he pulled from the dark recesses of his A level course mind and which was met with approval and agreement by all present. *Vraiment incroyable*. He took his leave, enjoying the short ride back to sit out in what was left of a fabulous sunset evening. Looking down at his watch, he realised that the meal had lasted seven hours, give or take.

Three Months In

That Saturday had seen a sea change in things for George on many fronts. Witnessing true Burgundian hospitality from a *vigneron* was immense, primed first by Tom and then by Marcel. He was beginning to think less about the vocabulary he did not know and work with what he had, picking up more along the way as he heard it in conversations. Perhaps more surprising than those, was the thought that he might actually enjoy female company again.

The misery and heartache left behind in the wake of Cathy's decision left him with a huge emptiness, which plagued his nights for weeks on end. It didn't feel wrong at the time, quite the opposite in fact, and coming to terms with it did not seem possible. Had he made a terrible mistake by forcing them both into a relationship through manipulation on his birthday? Or was this never going to go anywhere for any one of a number of reasons: impending departure for a year abroad being the most obvious, but perhaps religion or family expectations? All these things mounted up and added weight to a previously unburdened love. From it, he was left with a fear of female control over relationships which, it seemed, would always trump any male perspective he contemplated. It had all been overwhelming.

Work had helped of course, making new friends and testing out language skills was always a challenge. Through Dédé, he was introduced to his wife's good friend Geneviève and her boyfriend. Geneviève was a *vigneronne* with a vineyard out in Vosne, which of itself was amazing as one of the premier wines of the region. However it was talking to Dédé about his father's joining the RAF which prompted the introduction. Dédé knew Geneviève had a biplane, similar to the one George had heard about endlessly as a child: the celebrated Tiger Moth that his father had learnt to fly in.

On a bright, early afternoon in May he met them at a makeshift airfield just outside the town, which comprised rough grass, cut a little shorter than the surrounding wild grasses, against a backdrop of deciduous trees in full leaf by that time, making irregular shapes against an almost cloudless sky.

'Say hello to Midgy!' said Nicolas her boyfriend. For a moment George thought that he might be sharing his pet name for Geneviève with him, but thought that sharing a term of endearment was not likely at his first meeting. So he turned from looking in their direction to behind him, where a glorious red top half of a biplane stood, bright red tail and both wings were juxtaposed against a clean, white underbelly with a dramatic red flash below, the canopy pointing towards a single propeller. He noticed that the back of the canopy seemed to be wallpapered with a subtle and most decidedly feminine touch of a red diamond design. The canopy itself boasted long clear windows to the sides for optimal views left and right. He was glad to see that there was a clear sight of the propeller from the front-facing, cockpit window. He had noticed pictures of Cessna light aircraft before, where the engine cowling dominated the front and undoubtedly would impair the vision of the pilot. 'How would you ever see the ground beneath as you come into land?' was his first thought, but with this model everything seemed much more sensible.

'Hello Midgy. What a wonderful sight you are!' George greeted the biplane readily.

Now he realised why there was so much visibility and length, when the three of them climbed on board. Geneviève sat in the rear, while Nicolas sat with George up front. They climbed steadily after take-off and a thrill of exhilaration raced through George's veins, realising at once what had grabbed his father's attention all those years ago and why he continued to regale folks with his stories.

Glancing down at his feet, it was also evident why they had felt distinctly cooler than when they were on the ground. Gaps measuring between a few centimetres to an inch or more stared up at him, through which the trees and landscape below were as visible as if he had seen them through the canopy window to the side. He calmed himself in the comfort that this plane would have performed many flying hours without a hitch from well before he was born. Instead he looked out at the magnificent views of the vineyards stretching out before them: he recognised the monastic buildings alongside the château at Vougeot encircled by its distinctive walls, then heading north to Chambolle and Gevrey – whose wines George had begun to appreciate – before turning and heading back over the Hautes-Côtes de Nuits.

As they did so, Nicolas turned to George and asked, 'Want to have a go?' There was no hesitation in George's reply: *absolument*. For this his first time he was thrilled to take the controls, even just to go flat and level for a few minutes – or maybe it was seconds – before handing back control.

Geneviève's small stature belied her generosity. Cuddled up on the landing gear for a photo with Nicolas on the grass beside her, George could not help but admit that it was good to see relatively young people enjoying their time together. They seemed very together too.

So too he thought was the case at Paul's extended birthday lunch, where George had a great time chatting with his neighbour, Françoise, who had surprised him at their parting by making an arrangement to have a meal together the following weekend. George had wanted to cook and Françoise accepted.

He greeted her at the gate when the *clochette* rang, her diminutive form adorned with short, wavy hair, a small nose and a generous smile. She was quite sweet and the conversation flowed easily between them. George had started off with a tomato and frisée salad — thinking better of adding onions to the mix – with the dressing he had learnt from Babette drizzled over it. It was time to try it out on someone else for a second, independent opinion.

Françoise was generous in her praise, but was more thoughtful about the lamb's liver casserole with blackcurrant sauce he had prepared for a main. 'More of a man's dish', he quietly hummed to himself in the kitchen, while clearing away. He still had plenty of the *cubi* wine left but even there, she added a note of caution.

'You do know you're supposed to transfer that into individual bottles to make sure it doesn't go off, don't you?'

'Oh crap, really?' he pondered out loud. 'Ah well, there's nothing for it. I'll just have to drink it all before that happens. Will you help me make a start?' Françoise accepted the challenge, although rightly confining herself to a not too excessive amount of wine.

George looked at the *cubi* sat on the cool flagstones and said, 'I can't see any difference in the level, can you?' She agreed and proposed 'Do you mind me staying over, as I have work close by in the morning and I've had a bit too much to drink to drive home?'

'No, of course not', George said nonchalantly, 'There's an extra single bed in my room if you don't mind sharing a room.' They took turns in the small bathroom getting ready for bed. George settled down into his double bed before Françoise came in to take her place in the single. The lights were extinguished but the talking continued a little while longer. Then Françoise asked curiously after a longer pause, which George assumed would be the precursor to sleep, 'Do you not have a little space in your big bed for me?' He didn't need any translator for that and opened up his side of the covers for her to slip under.

She cuddled up to him for warmth; they kissed passionately and made love in short order. Making sure she wasn't late for work, George went out for fresh croissants and made coffee. In a trice, she was out the gate and gone.

'That was interesting,' he mused, 'Didn't know that would happen.' With the passing of another day, his dream featured a very graphic Françoise with him in bed, exploring each other in anticipation of a next meeting. But that was not to come. He was not unduly surprised, as his performance that night had not been good, but he continued to dream… this time in French! He had reached the third stage he concluded, and with that, he sat down and penned a short poem entitled *La clochette qui ne sonne pas*. He felt he was moving on… finally.

Heading Out and About

No more than three weeks later, another invitation to picnic in the countryside came about and sitting at a picnic table, he felt sure that a lady called Anne-Marie was flirting with him. They had only just met. He wondered seriously if he had switched to wearing another after shave or deodorant, but no, that was not it. He left without making any arrangements, fearing he may have misunderstood the language used or the situation.

His attention then turned to his former fellow students who had made the journey across the Channel into this brave new, or not so new, world. Many complained of being bored to tears, by having to attend lectures so many hours a week and not really being able to practice French that much outside of classes. George suddenly felt lucky for the opportunities that had been put before him, for the first time.

To cheer them up, he arranged to travel at weekends to meet up and catch up.

Leo it turned out had found work on the outskirts of Paris which took up all his time, so George turned to Lou, who had landed a cool spot, quite literally, in Evian-les-Bains, close enough to visit the slopes of Meribel. Her work was not as a ski resort manager but at a school. Her only disappointment was realising that, as a spa town, nothing much happened there in the off-peak season, so most of the houses there were shuttered up as were a lot of the supporting businesses.

She survived better than the rest due to her willingness to talk to anyone, which was fast becoming a trait she shared with George.

In fact, at Victoria Station once before this year abroad, he had been seeing Leo off back to Kent when they encountered a Swiss girl and her friend on the platform and got talking to them. In a matter of ten minutes only, she and George knew that they had much more they could discuss with each other, but time was incredibly short. So they exchanged addresses – in the UK and Switzerland first, then in France later – and from the outset, there flowed between them a huge amount of regular correspondence in a mixture of languages over that year. Both had repeated in their letters to each other many times the phrase 'Can you believe this? After only a few minutes on a platform together?'

George often wondered if they would meet up or be more than friends, but she acted more as consolation to George's loneliness. He confided much in her, but withheld details of his unhappiness to preserve both her sanity and their friendship. He guessed that it showed through occasionally, though he tried to hide it.

On his trip to see Lou, she introduced him to two good friends of hers, neither romantically involved with her: René and Armand. They hailed from Marseille. How they met he did not recall, but it was a strange coincidence to see those polar extremes of temperature come together in the one location. No one had skis with them and, being too expensive to hire, they contented themselves with playing an impromptu football game, kicking around a piece of ice. They both were great fun and Lou's effervescence shone through at all times. She was indestructible and always a sound friend to George.

The two *Marseillais* were very entertaining and invited George to spend a weekend down at their flat in Marseille which he accepted willingly. He took in the view of that sprawling city from the heights of Notre Dame de la Garde and wondered at the sheer expanse of city in front of him. They showed him the spectacular coastline and drove him inland into Le Midi, where public water wells provided much-needed refreshment and shade from the sun. He also took away how to marinate rabbit in Mediterranean herbs and vegetables overnight, which was a fabulous bonus.

On another occasion, he travelled south to Lyon to catch up with three girls from the French set, who had clearly decided to stick together in the same location and same university, but were pretty lacklustre about their experience thus far. The ornate cathedral and museum with its classical frontage were interesting enough, but only for a tourist visiting for the weekend, as George was.

It was strange running into the only girlfriend – if you could call her that – he had during his first year. Kate and George had seemed drawn to one another through height alone, both thinking that people of their size would naturally get along just fine. They were both wrong.

It wasn't all one-way traffic. George hosted more than one visitor back at his home. Rhiannon had come over with a German exchange student, doing much the same as her, but from Heidelberg University. Rhiannon was a good friend back at Uni, always ready to listen and found the same things hilariously amusing. This included the endless pranks George and the other two carried out during the first two years there. She was from the north-west of England, very much a Welsh girl at heart and refreshingly down to earth with flaming, natural red hair in a petite frame. Nothing much would stop her once she had made a commitment. This was exemplified by her visit, as a passenger to her German buddy, since she had broken her arm just a few days before, but refused to cancel.

It was the end of May now and looming large was the possibility of returning to Uni for the June ball, but there was one slight problem: George had no one to go with!

Lou had already said she would not go: lack of transport and funds prohibited her from attending. Of the other two close friends, Harriet was a non-starter, as George wasn't sure if she had overcome her acute shyness of men. Probably not. So he reached out to Berenice and he was quite pleasantly surprised when she accepted.

Now that was settled, he got in touch with Paul and Agnès, as he promised to let them know if he was ever going to return to the UK. They both jumped at the chance and dropped everything to plan their trip. They just wanted to hitch a lift across the Channel to London. Easy enough you'd think, but little did they know what the trip had planned for them.

Butterfly Wide Open

George had made a couple of trips back to the UK already and knew it would take roughly fourteen hours door to door for him. He took the red *route nationale* roads to avoid the tolls, a less smooth ride under the wheels – as government funding was concentrated on maintaining motorways – but it was far more interesting and he got to see the real France.

He was also used to going through the centre of Paris, timing it to coincide with the early morning flushing of the streets with water pumped up from the Seine, which gave the city its fresh and clean look along its stunning boulevards. Even the *Place de l'Etoile* was a joy to go around at 4am he thought. However, with passengers who might not appreciate the unsociable hours he kept when driving, he proposed going around Paris instead. The only disadvantage was that they would now be hitting the now infamous *periphérique* ring road during rush hour to make the ferry on time.

Travelling up through the stunning regional park of Morvan, passing through Avallon, stopping off at Auxerre, before motoring on in the little red *coccinelle*, they were having a great time feasting on the sights and on the charcuterie they had brought along for the journey. Everyone was on a budget but enjoying the ride.

Having travelled once before round the Paris ring road with his sister and boyfriend, George remembered that it was just a simple case of taking the right *porte* exit, but what happened next he had not planned for.

It was about half three in the afternoon, when they arrived at the *Porte d'Italie* and joined the fast-moving stream of vehicles charging along what is now the inner ring road. George thought he was looking for Clignancourt or Chapelle to exit onto the N1 which would take them north to Calais. Paul, who had become the navigator, agreed.

They had only gone a few hundred metres past the Saint-Cloud exit, when George pressed a little harder on the accelerator to move past a slower-moving long vehicle. Suddenly, the car lurched forwards under its own steam and stormed past vehicle after vehicle, while George was trying to brake on and off to temper the insane acceleration which had kicked off moments earlier. 'What's happening?' cried out Paul, 'Can't you brake to slow us down?'

Exits at Villiers, Clignancourt and Chaumont all passed by before George could answer.

'Yes I am braking, but it's no use. She just keeps accelerating and at this rate the brakes will overheat and seize up if this keeps on going.'

'Do something George,' pleaded Agnès from the back seat, 'or we're going to die. Good God!' There was panic and George had to think quickly.

'Alright. Here's what I'm going to do…' he shouted to make himself heard above the noise of the screaming engine, 'the next exit we come to, I'm gonna throw it into neutral, the revs will go sky high and I'll cut the engine. Hopefully we can drift to a junction and take it from there. OK?'

'You're the driver George. Go for it', Paul replied nervously, the tones in his voice noticeably wishing it would end safely.

Exit Saint-Cloud passed them at speed for a second time. 'Right. We're coming off at the next exit.' The slip road came into view after the road veered quite severely to the right, more severely than last time due to the massive speed hike. 'Ok. Here goes.'

He slipped it out of gear and the revs immediately went through the roof. The noise was deafening. Feeling down to his right below the steering wheel, he turned the ignition off. The silence now was drowned out by the previous engine noise still resonating in their ears. There was a gasp from both his passengers.

He had chosen badly. The exit road was miniscule. A short ramp, no more than fifty metres long, climbed up steeply to a set of traffic lights, which were red!

George slammed on the brakes and pulled on the handbrake too which pulled them up just in time to cross the white line of the lights.

Again thinking ahead, he put on the advance warning lights and ordered 'Everyone out. We need to push.' The car was still on a bit of a slope and with traffic coming off behind them, it was dangerous to stay where they were.

With the two pushing at the rear and George pushing with the driver's door open, he turned the wheel to the right to cross the lights before pulling over to their left onto a smaller road, where it came to rest against the kerb. Looking around he couldn't believe they were in the middle of what appeared to be a wood. Never expecting this, he asked 'Where are we?'

'It said the Bois de Boulogne on the exit board.' answered Paul.

Agnès slumped down into the driver's seat, relieved to have come to a halt with no one hurt, just shaken. 'Well, what shall we do now?' asked a more than worried Paul. 'How are we going to get to London by tonight?'

'Well, that's not going to happen', retorted George sharply, having come from one traumatic incident to be projected straight into another, without a break or thought for what had just happened.

'Let me call the International breakdown service first. Then I'll get on to the ferry company.' The news was not good on the breakdown service front. No one was available until the following morning at 8am, so that was it. They were stuck there for the night. With no funds to afford even a two-star hotel, they resorted to what they had brought with them in the car.

George was the only one to have brought a sleeping bag with him for emergency purposes; the other two had prearranged accommodation, so nothing doing there.

'Ok. What I suggest,' declared George like a CO with no other options before him,' is you sleep in the car Agnès, and lock both doors. We'll just be outside, not too far away. There's a plastic sheet we can put down on the ground a little way from the car into the woodland area. Paul and I will have to share the double sleeping bag. Is that okay for you both?'

The others agreed seeing that that was probably the safest if not only solution. Neither of them had been to Paris ever before, even on school trips. And George thought *he* was from the country!

They ate what remained of the snacks they had brought with them, choosing to wait till the car was fixed before searching out breakfast croissant or coffee, as there was nothing in the immediate vicinity which looked remotely like civilisation.

'I can't believe we're in Paris and there's nowhere to eat,' sighed Paul in disappointment. We must have stopped in the only place in Paris where there's nothing to eat or drink!'

Moose Conquering Fear

George resisted the temptation to turn on Paul's comments or join him in bemoaning their fate. 'Well, I don't know about you two,' he said wearily, 'but I've had more than enough excitement for one day. I'm going to get my head down.'

Darkness was already upon them. Agnès made herself as comfortable as possible, stretched out on the back seat covered by a blanket George always carried with him. By the dim glow of the courtesy light in the car, the two young men hunkered down to the sides of the generously proportioned blue sleeping blanket, under a tree no more than ten metres from the car.

The air was crisp but still and the ground around them bare rather than grassy, with many twigs broken off from the tree scattered about them. They drifted off into a deep slumber almost immediately.

The noise of breaking twigs stirred George, who became suddenly awake and alert to possible danger. 'Wake up Paul!' he said in a loud whisper, 'The car light is on.' They scrambled to their feet and could see the interior of the car lit up. It was empty; the passenger side door, wide open.

'Where's Agnès?' Paul's voice trembled, then more forcefully shouted out, 'Agnès!' A dark, tousled hair figure ran towards them.

'I'm not staying a minute longer in the car.' protested a distraught Agnès, 'There are men going round and round the car tapping on the windows and making rude suggestions to me.'

'Oh you poor thing', comforted Paul, giving his sister the biggest of hugs.

'Is that sleeping bag big enough for three?' her voice pleading desperately for it to be true.

'I'm sure it can, as there's not much to any of us. We're all pretty thin', assessed George correctly. With the car now locked up, they settled down like comfortable sardines and nodded off quickly in the safety of being together.

To their surprise they missed dawn and slept on amply into the early morning. Paul went off in search of coffee and croissants, while the other two packed up the bedding. It wasn't long before a bright yellow van pulled over behind their car. 'Automobile Assistance to the rescue', George hoped, 'If they just tow us to a garage, that would be great but could mean more delays and we might miss our ferry. Let's see what he has to say.'

Butterfly Wide Open

Fortunately for them the hero had come fully prepared and began dismantling the carburettor before their eyes. Within a few minutes, he pronounced 'You've had a lucky escape, that's for sure.'

He held up a small right angled metal pipe no bigger than his thumbnail, 'See that? That injects fuel into your carburettor.'

George looked at it wondering if it needed a replacement and whether he would have such a part in his van. Surely he did not carry all parts for all vehicles in his small van. That ferry was not getting any closer. His underarms started to ache and break out into what he recognised as a nervous, cold sweat from his schooldays.

'It has popped out – it's not supposed to – and wedged the butterfly wide open.' George knew enough about engines from helping his father to realise how dangerous that was, and why he had been unable to do anything about it on the ring road only a few hours before.

'I say lucky,' continued the service man, 'because if that had fallen down through the gap and past the butterfly, there is nothing to stop it going all the way down into the engine and breaking the head.' The full gravity of what might have been now struck all of them. 'Can it be fixed?' asked Paul tentatively, George remaining speechless for several moments. 'Yes', came the comforting reply, 'There you go', he said banging it back in with force, 'That's not coming out again, ever. Start her up.'

On the second pump of the throttle, the red beetle coughed into life and her bodywork seemed to gleam now in the sunlight, which penetrated the trees above them, as she settled down into the familiar, rhythmic pulse George knew well.

Explaining their need to get on the road, they thanked the gentleman for saving their skins and were on their way.

The car posed no further troubles, taking George to the June ball, enjoyable to share with Berenice again but fairly unremarkable as an event, before ferrying all three back across the Channel a few days later with no unanticipated interruptions or incidents.

Singing a New Song

Emerging from the ferry onto the now familiar right-hand side of the road, George felt a glad reunion, as if he was missing this second homeland more on the return journey. The avenues of trees along country roads welcomed him back, with no explanation as to why they had been planted miles from any settlement, other than to please a visiting traveller's eye.

The *villes fleuries* through which he passed boasted their amazing floral pageants at the entrance and exit of every home town, forcing him to slow down and pay more particular attention to each. He could take in the delicate interwoven mix of floral tributes, pollarded plane trees and gravel *boule* strips or squares, where the wily characters of that place – young and old – always seemed to congregate. There was certainly more to look forward to, when he arrived on the other side of the Channel.

Through Tom, he had joined the *Chorale de Beaune*, a short trip from Nuits on a Tuesday night. He had always enjoyed singing, from church choir stall as a nine year old to singing Beethoven's ninth in the cathedral with full orchestra under the baton of an inimitable conductor called Anthony and performing Palestrina's Stabat Mater, echoing alternate responses between both chancels.

This smaller choir, of no more than twenty singers, brought together people from different walks of adult life, to celebrate local Burgundian folk tunes and those folk and dance melodies from the conductor's home country of Yugoslavia. Mateja was an inspiration, producing all the choral manuscripts himself, lovingly prepared in their original native tongue in a wide-brush hand, with a helpful French translation beneath.

He assisted in the pronunciation of course, but it was his feeling for a life past, wrapped up in nostalgic appeal of everyday occurrences – expressing an appreciation and devotion to his country which was overwhelming – that caught them all up in what was nothing less than a choral trance. That love of country was depicted in songs such as *Oj Moravo*, an immensely enjoyable irregularly rhythmed dance from southern Serbia, *Sto Mi Je Milo* and an enchanting religious plainsong from the Serbian liturgy *Mironosicam Zenam*.

Being a long-time resident of the Beaune region, he gladly presented the choir at concerts, at religious venues and on tour. He also respected the many French traditions of the calendar. So on twelfth night, as George knew it, he

Singing a New Song

was introduced to the *galette des rois* or rather two *galettes* which he would not have seen eaten in an English choir, for fear of straining the diaphragm with excessive food.

These *galettes* were essentially apple tarts with firm but pale, ribbed pastry topped with apple slices, layered to perfection, their leading edges a dazzling brown like burnished gold. George felt himself drooling at the very sight of them… and he was not alone.

He gathered that tradition has it, that each shall take a portion – the men from one tart and the ladies from the other. Inside the cake there was held a symbol of royalty which, when found, made the recipient into the king or queen for the evening.

At this point, George recalled very vividly sitting down at his nan's one Christmas and having the spotlight turned on him, as he complained about a hard object in his pudding: turned out to be a silver sixpence, although it didn't look much like it, being covered in a brown residue, that was as hard to rub off the coin as it was to remove from between his teeth. He conceded later that there was some fun to be had from the exercise as well as being a welcome addition to his pocket money. He only wished he had been warned beforehand.

No problems on that score on this occasion however. It wasn't long before his tongue found what seemed like a plastic icon or effigy in his mouth. He carefully wiped it clean to reveal a crown. *Félicitations*, they all cried out, 'And here is your Queen for the evening.' He turned to see Geneviève holding a similar coronet on her outstretched hand, which she invited him to take.

'The first dance is ours I believe', she said coyly.

'Oh? Dance?' acting pleasantly surprised as he did, 'Music maestro. Shall we?' Remembering a little from seeing his parents waltz within their small sitting room – trying to impart the moves to his elder brother and sister many times over – he took Geneviève in his arms and they danced gently around the room. This had been, he thought, the first time he had danced in front of an impromptu audience since pantomime plays at primary school, where dancing was called for and, on one occasion, bad singing in the title role of Sinbad the Sailor. Only decades later did he realise this must have been the producer's attempt at word play or poor humour. However, it did end well: memorably because he did end up getting the girl, albeit only on stage for a brief second that they kissed, before retreating a metre away from each other.

George started to wonder if the same outcome was expected at the end of this dance or towards the end of the evening. He thought he would pre-empt both by kissing Geneviève gently on both cheeks as per the regular custom and twice for good measure for close friends.

Geneviève seemed pleased at the ending, a not unattractive lady of middle years whose brightly floral dress had caught his eye earlier on in the proceedings. The party concluded with Geneviève arranging to meet up again with the group in the market square of Nuits the following weekend.

Not everyone made it to what was billed as an open market event with music and wine flowing, cheese tastings and other culinary delights. The day was beautifully warm. Turning towards the belfry as he sensed he ought to, the fine figure in a low cut square neckline turned the corner to reveal Geneviève and her ample cleavage looking right at him.

They chatted, sometimes nervously on George's part, touring the assembled stalls and tasting their wares and flavours. George's palette was improving by this time. He now limited himself to sampling wine only when preceded by a sliver of *gruyère* to bring out the flavours more. It was remarkable – as Tom had alluded to right from the outset – that every village on the Côte possessed different qualities and flavours due to the subtle changes in soil composition. That is why he had purchased his own vineyards in the area to advance the possibility of, one day, owning and producing a wine fit enough to be deemed and certified as *appellation controlée* and perhaps be good enough to be admitted to the *Confrérie des Chevaliers du Tastevin*. He wasn't holding his breath however.

They had spoken together on the back seats of a coach when going on tour with the choir once about Geneviève. She cut an isolated figure at the back of the coach, but he thought much was simmering beneath which needed to surface. He wasn't wrong.

Geneviève beckoned George over towards the close of the afternoon, once most of the stalls were packing up, to invite him to see her vineyard down in Meursault. 'There's a particular vine I want to show you.' He didn't know quite what to make of this, but went along for the white grape vineyard experience as the evening was promising a fine sunset.

Arriving in amongst vines higher than those in Nuits – as they were on taller trellises two metres or so apart – he wondered, 'How do you spray these? Are your tractors extra tall?' He had noted the commonplace blue tractors which straddle a single vine, but their clearance height was limited.

'We have tractors that fit between the vines and can service the vines on either side. It's more efficient', came the comprehensive reply.

'No arguing with that for sure', he thought, 'This is a smart lady who knows her trade as well as being able to hold a scintillating soprano line.'

They enjoyed staying behind after the chorale had finished to practise a duet Mateja had wished for them to sing. She was outstanding and blended in well with his own baritone-cum-tenor-cum-counter-tenor range, developed over many years as he slid inexorably down the scale, holding on to higher voices as he went. He counted himself very lucky in this.

Now too as they spoke in the calmness of her car as the sun sank slowly from the sky, they seemed at one with the vines, the windows slightly open conveying a light breeze that played with her fair hair. As she pulled it to clear her face, they embraced fully and longingly as though there had been a long wait for this to happen. They both felt it.

He learnt more explicit language than he had ever done before with Geneviève. She introduced him to the subtle linguistic difference between *baissable* and *baisable* car seats while they lay flat beside each other. Although it was never his intention to ever smoke, he nonetheless learnt the meaning too of *fumer la pipe*, the finer points of which she had no hesitation in showing him.

Their encounter only lasted a few weeks for two reasons. Sumptuous as she was, George was disconcerted when she took him back to her house once, when her then partner occupied the same house. That was incredibly awkward and was an experience he did not want to repeat again... ever.

Secondly, and more importantly, he had run into a young girl of his own age, quite by chance later the next month. She was bubbly, effervescent, unstoppable in many ways and charming. She had the habit of tilting her head to one side when she admired George's efforts to converse or made her laugh. Her brown hair was straight and very short, which complemented her serious task of embarking on studies in Paris, already undertaken the previous autumn.

She was the daughter of a local *vigneron* – almost inevitably in this place where it seemed more and more likely to George, the more people he met – tucked away just a little way up the hill across the other side of the Meuzin. A short walk from his own digs as luck would have it. She too had shown him her father's vines, but preferred him to experience a light show better than any *son-et-lumière* he had ever seen. They approached a hedge in the late evening no more than fifty metres to the rear of her house to see it bespattered with what looked like green luminescent paint, but were in fact dozens and dozens of glow-worms. Agnès, another one not Paul's sister, expanded his knowledge with the insight that these were all females attracting a mate. How wonderful and how personal she made that sound.

Her family were most welcoming too. They had another younger daughter, an adopted son from the Orient and a wonderfully extrovert son, Jean-Luc, who may have had learning difficulties but his directness was a breath of fresh air, loved by the whole family. They were a genuinely loving family, even though the grandfather would give disapproving looks when Jean-Luc appeared to ruin a photo or make an inappropriate remark. The rest of them just laughed, including his grandmother who tolerated everyone and everything to do with them.

Theirs was a much more rewarding match than previous encounters, which had all been brief or lacking substance. George visited Agnès in Paris at her accommodation on the third floor: so many steps carrying suitcases up the traditional spiral wooden staircase with black iron railings, but oozing with the character of the thousands of feet that had climbed – as they now did – over centuries before them. The tiny quarters were just large enough to fit a desk and single bed in, into which they snuggled down for the night in dangerously but willingly close proximity.

The relationship was George's longest and extended beyond his return to his country of origin, where he resumed his final year at university. They called each other regularly, both visited each other once and Agnès got to meet George's remaining friends still at college as well as some of the French set who had returned.

The final year became loaded with work as expected and the calls diminished. No more visits were possible until after the end of the summer term at the very earliest. Agnès resorted to writing letters once a week that were answered initially, but became impossible to commit time to as the second and third terms wore on.

Singing a New Song

The more the situation went on, the darker the letters became. Accusations and questions about the strength of their love at a distance became more and more pressing to the point that George's heart sank when he saw another blue airmail letter in his pigeonhole in the JCR.

The situation was untenable and he wanted to escape, but in college there was only one place close enough to do that without overly disrupting studies and that was the college bar.

Turning to drink was not a commendable course of action, which resulted in an event and a night which he would come to rue years later.

Love the One you're with

'Hello, who's this then?' asked Dave, George's neighbour in Thropp House, the hall of residence where Leo and George had decided to sit out their final year. Seemed like a good idea at the time: all found, dining room nearby, library too – though that did not concern them greatly – short walk to the bar and staggerable home as it was all downhill. Perfect… or so they thought. Stu had not joined them but stayed in the Gilsperch lodging, somehow managing to apply for and be accepted onto a Master's degree in Economics, thus guaranteeing that he'd be there when the other two returned, for which they were very grateful.

Dave was hanging his head out of the window when he'd made the remark. It was aimed at the young girl who had also decided to hang her head out of George's window at the same time. Her bedraggled hair and scant attire told Dave all he needed to know. Introductions were made in full earshot of all forty other windows on the riverside front of that building, which echoed to the sound of a similar question as each window opened, till all were satisfied that acquaintances had been made. They made their way to breakfast to recount the night's events that led up to that revelation.

Dave used to enjoy telling the story of how this happened one morning and continued to be the case every morning right up to the end of the summer term.

It was more than George had expected to happen and the fallout was immense.

About the same time, Leo happened upon a girl – or rather Kayleigh happened upon him as he always struggled to fathom out girls in general or any girlfriend in particular – and a match was made. More through convenience – as both girls hailed from the Crispin block in that part of the college – than ardent desire, the couples made up a four in the early days to get to know each other, enjoy some downtime together and meet up from time to time. They could not relax of course and sometimes this boiled over.

George remembered one evening when walking back from the bar, how he had been piqued particularly by the behaviour of his new found partner, Mel, when she seemed to flirt extensively and he thought excessively with other men in the bar.

He blamed himself for this insecurity, believing it to be perhaps a throwback to his previous parting experience or maybe a reaction to the guilt he felt at leaving Agnès in the lurch, especially with her being so far away. It seemed to him that the old adage was true: long-distance relationships did not work. Although there were times when he wished it would have done.

As they were descending the slope back to Thropp and for no reason, George blurted some abuse out in French, which involved Greeks and began *va te faire…* aimed at his new partner. The only person to fully understand this was of course Leo. His face contorted to a shocked but stifled surprise with lips closed. 'Must be the drink talking', Leo offered by way of excuse to the girls following on behind. But George meant it. Something had changed, he pondered later, and he didn't like it.

The same faces greeted Dave outside the window the next morning and life continued by default.

Within one week or so, George knew he had to tell Agnès about this new situation. He called her from an empty JCR on the only call booth, while the rest were at tea. It was 5pm and the light was fading, not because of the time, but because the only windows were way up next to the ceiling and light could not find its way easily into that space.

There were moans and tears on one end of the phone and suppressed, humiliated damp eyes at the other. He hated doing it, but it had to be done. 'I don't deserve you. You're better off without me, you really are Agnès', came the feeble excuse for a man that George had become.

By the end of twenty minutes or so, her quick mind closed the call by reminding him of an artist's song they both had shared and admired together during their time. Now though it had added meaning, induced more heartache and left them both with a sense of hopelessness with it all. 'Remember: you can 'Love the One you're with', but it may not be the right one.' With that she hung up the phone and his life became the poorer for it.

Doing Just Enough

Spotting flaws in a relationship was not a skill George possessed. His weakness was to carry on regardless, hoping that everything would turn out for the best, whichever way the wind blew. He was dejected for some considerable time after the break with Agnès. Even his closest female friend Lou expressed surprise and regret 'That's a shame. I thought she was a really nice girl. I liked her.'

In the first few weeks after his return from France, he thought he was getting better at spotting emotional traps, such as the one set by an ex-girlfriend from his first year. She had invited both Leo and himself out with two or three French set friends for an evening meal to catch up. Kate had only one purpose which was obvious when inviting him to her room for coffee later. There was a timely interruption by one of her friends who lived opposite and was clearly in the know. While Kate dealt with the intrusion, she had left the door open enough for her words to filter through, leaving an echo in his head, 'Can't you see you're cramping my style!' With that he left her room, leaving the door deliberately wider open than he'd found it and made his way quickly but quietly out of the building without uttering a word.

Now he paid limited attention to both Mel and friends. He reflected sorrowfully on how he had had to pick up the pieces on arriving in France and now he had done the same thing to another human being. All manner of decency had deserted him, he concluded.

Acquiescing to the occasional, sober evening out, he threw himself into his studies for the remaining term time as they all had to.

That summer was less of a celebration than previous ones and tinged with sadness: filling their days with deep and meaningful conversations with Lou, Harriet, Leo and Stu – Berenice having gone down the year before after their summer ball together – and making plans to meet up during the holidays. And meet up they did: the Nag's Head was a regular hostelry they all reconvened at. Lou was driving a red Volvo by then and visited George's house, bringing with him Berenice and Harriet. They seemed to enjoy meeting his parents, walking round the village and looking in at The Lamb, before posing for a photo in front of the Blacksmith's pond.

Back at Uni, the results were out and tutors called them in for a concluding chat and farewell. George had the same lady tutor consistently throughout and her comments were amusing but telling:

'Well, you have joined the swelling ranks of the 2.2s. You are not alone in this set. I can't recall seeing so many in one year group.' adding by way of reprimand falling short of outright condemnation, 'Seems to me… you all did just enough!' She paused before continuing, 'But I guess you all had a damn good time of it, while you were here.'

'You could say that.' he managed to squeeze out without adding any further elaboration and showed himself out of the door after a brief goodbye.

'Well now that's over, all we have to do is find a job!' said Leo as they both emerged from the riverside building. 'Yes, that could be a tough one. Haven't really thought too much about that.' replied George. Stu was still ensconced in revision as his Masters exams were well beyond the end of term. Nonetheless, he joined in their conversation about futures, which for him had changed from the Hong Kong police force to working for the Bank of England.

'You know you can't take your work home with you, if you work for them, don't you?' George posed ruefully, ribbing Stu who snickered at the thought before replying 'No, but I could try, couldn't I.'

Leo revealed a plan to join the Baltic Exchange, which seemed to have been withheld from their chats for a while, from the sheepish look on his face. 'Ok. Well that's you two sorted. I'll just have to wait and see what is out there, once I decide what I want to do.' George added airily and without much purpose.

As it happened, he would not have to wait and see for long.

A call was taken in the JCR and it was his former French teacher from primary school. Her lilting Welsh accent had not altered in the intervening years. She came to the point succinctly.

'I've decided to give up my French teaching position at a day and boarding school down in Surrey and wondered if you'd be interested in becoming my replacement. You'd have to come down for an interview of course.'

This was music to his ears. An opportunity put on the very plate in front of him. This, he thought, must be his destiny. Who would have thought it? It's a shame Leo had already gone down, but he shared his news with Stu.

'Of course I'd love to be considered. What are you moving on to, may I ask, if it's not a secret?'

Moose Conquering Fear

'Oh, James and I want to open a tea room on the Suffolk coast. Well, mostly me I suppose, but he's game and up for it.'

With that, they made the arrangements and before the end of the summer, the job was his.

Surrey Days

If George thought it was a bit of a shock being given an opportunity so quickly, it was an even bigger shock for his mum who, he learnt a few years later, was dumbstruck that her youngest was moving away to start a job in the September following his return in July.

'Well, I don't want to be a burden to you both and I will pay you back for the car as soon as I get settled in and get my first pay cheques.' This was his excuse for moving on with his life, an idea which was even stronger after a year abroad and the independence it brought.

He didn't pay off the car immediately, preferring to spend almost all of his first month's cheque on a then state-of-the-art stereo Hi-Fi system with turntable, tape deck, radio and two speakers. This would prove invaluable in the single room he was allocated at the school as the tool of choice for waking up boarders during his one-in-three, week on duty. The other two weeks being filled with either classical music from one confirmed bachelor, who was George's immediate neighbour or by silence with the occasional shrieks, as resistant students were tipped out of their beds and dumped unceremoniously on the floor by another confirmed bachelor. It came as much-needed relief to their ears when George was on wake-up duty or so he was told. For them, when the air and corridors were filled with the addictive drumbeats of Adam Ant reverberating up and down stairs, it merely served to emphasise that the younger generation were now in charge.

The room he had been allocated was pleasant enough: warm, a single bed, desk looking out over a flat roof to the chapel across the way with the fruit trees from the adjoining orchard almost reaching the chapel door.

Being in-house had its benefits as well as a few downsides. The main dormitory opposite his room was directly above the dining room and only a short walk therefore to the kitchen and an awaiting milky coffee, bacon sandwich and the cheeriest of smiles from Kaleah, who also lived on site and worked under Jean, the head cook.

They took good care of him and thoroughly spoiled him during his time, as they did other regulars who gave the time of day to talk with the kitchen staff. The whole staff did not indulge in this activity, which George advertised out loud on more than one occasion: 'Best start to the day, ever.'

Moose Conquering Fear

Throwing himself into a boarding life was at once strange, amusing and enjoyable.

Strange, because he had never experienced it himself. The closest he came to it was his childhood friend who lived quite close to him in the large, Elizabethan thatched house at the end of the road. He was almost always in uniform and being driven dozens of miles to and from school most days, it seemed. As such, time was always limited and the friendship could not therefore blossom as it otherwise might have. He seemed even at that young age to be from a different world to his own.

Amusing, because of the eccentric nature of some of the teaching staff. One, from the very same university as himself had studied Divinity, preceding him easily by at least three decades. His coiffure, or lack of it, belied his studies since there remained just the fringe of what had presumably been a thick crop of hair, with the busiest and widest of ring roads in a circular expanse on top, leaving nothing but the distinct impression of having led a cloistered life.

Another was regularly mistaken as the gardener due to the rather dishevelled nature of his checked jacket, which never changed until the threadbare parts overwhelmed the weave to the extent that the elbow patches seemed to keep the whole ensemble together by good fortune. When a change of attire did take place, as George witnessed only once at the end of a four year stint, the wearer explained he had purchased a job lot of the same jacket when he first took up his post as an economy. Too proud perhaps to acknowledge that this now resembled more a false economy than a sound investment, he contented himself with finishing others' diverse attempts at completing the Telegraph crossword of a weekend or of an evening when time permitted. Given the amount of time during and after school and during weekends that he devoted to the school – including cleaning the shoes of boys who were either too reticent or forgetful to do the same – it should be no surprise that this was the very embodiment of what a Deputy Head at a boys' private school should be. A yardstick which was never surpassed and to whom George owed a huge debt of gratitude for introducing him to the concept of 'knowing your Onions'. No ordinary meaning of knowing your profession or a particular skill, but a nod to the immense undertaking which is the reference book of Etymology, written by a man of the same name.

Lastly, it was enjoyable for the unfathomable joy that imparting ways of learning, reasoning and discovery could bring in a genuine bidirectional learning curve that being first a schoolmaster of French, then Mathematics and eventually IT instruction involved.

In this open and creative environment, the luxury of having sport every day meant that the same techniques could be applied equally to the sports field, much to the delight of the youngest Game 8 as they were referred to. Some educators saw taking that age group of seven to eight year olds for sport as not far removed from babysitting, but to the more enlightened among them, they were the cradle where great things could be nurtured. So it was that they and some of the other teaching staff were amazed to find that the same drills and techniques used for the 1st and 2nd XI teams were being shared with these youngsters. George saw it as a requisite investment of time for future sporting excellence.

From the very first day, he had hit upon a phrase credited to Plato which he inscribed on card and hung it over the entrance door to his classroom, which stated clearly for all teaching conducted in that place,

> Do not train a child to learn by force or harshness; but direct them to it by what amuses their minds, so that you may be better able to discover with accuracy the peculiar bent of the genius of each.

Led too by an inspirational Head – a former Treasury official whose way with words was a shining example of communication in all matters but particularly with parents – he could rightfully say that these years were among his happiest.

One gem of advice he learnt from the Head on replying to any correspondence: 'Always mention in the first line your thanks "for the letter received *today*." The promptness of your considered reply will bode well in all future correspondence and, for the most part, elicit a timely follow up to any request made subsequently in your letter.' A lesson he never forgot.

It was easy to become wrapped up in an all-inclusive world such as this. He met some great people from kitchen staff to matrons to teaching and gardening staff, four years passing like four months.

It was hard to cultivate any relationship with his girlfriend from college as she entered her fourth and final year of teacher training, especially with the sleeping arrangements in-house, so to speak. One visit saw her rise late, only to be spotted by a younger male, married teacher as she exited the only bathroom, which was situated inconveniently right next to the staff common room. Dressed in a black, full length, silky-looking negligée with buxom bosom partially exposed, his inappropriate comment of 'She looks fit' sealed it for George, who requested a move out of the school in his second year.

It must be said that the school were not overly generous in their first offer, which was a one-bedroom flat above a retail parade of shops in the village square. Though only a 20 minute slow walk to the school, the flat was accessed by a small, previously invisible gate which opened with difficulty and showed significant signs of rusting, even on the handle.

The owner met him on the other side, a short elderly woman in her seventies he would say, with a hairdresser hairdo salvaged from the few remaining fine hairs that old age inflicts mercilessly on many. She had a pleasant disposition and was quite welcoming. 'Lovely to see it occupied again.' she said, trusting there would be few questions that followed on. 'Well, go on in. You'll find the door at the top of the stairs to your left. I'll leave you to wander.'

'Mi legs ain't what they used to be, yer know', she added putting George at ease, as she slipped seamlessly into her usual voice and accent.

The door resisted a little but gave way under a gentle shoulder barge. His eye caught the cream fridge: hard to tell if that was its original or acquired colour. It was light enough under a pitched roof and warm already at 9am in an early summer. The windows opened which was something, but as he crossed the floor a crunching sound underfoot first offended his ears and then drew his gaze down to floor level. He pulled up short. The worn pale green carpet had ridges normally associated with the hard-wearing, office kind. No surprises there, but the rills were grey-black not with dust in even lines but in blotches which covered the carpet from one side to the other. Closer inspection revealed behind him that he had trodden on an infestation of bluebottle and house flies, none of them fresh and all of them desiccated by months if not years of heat and neglect.

He went no further into the room, but tentatively called out from within, 'Is there a vacuum cleaner?'

'Oh yes, my dear,' she announced with confidence, 'just in the cupboard under the eaves.'

'This has to be like running a medieval gauntlet', he thought as he measured with his eyes, calculating the distance between him and the cupboard to be about five metres. He scrunched his way as quickly and as humanely as possible to that side, opening the door. He was wrong about the old lady – it was the vacuum cleaner that was the oldest thing in the room. He had seen recreations of

Victorian living rooms in northern museums: this relic predated those by a long chalk. Its two four-inch, contra-rotating rotary brushes he was confident would accomplish nothing but pass the offending detritus through the machine and out the other side, avoiding the bag placed loosely over the base completely.

'Have to bring my own I think', he shouted out to be heard and then quipped, 'This one belongs in a museum.' There was no reply.

He knuckled down to the clean up over the summer, but worse was to come. The contents of his fridge began to smell within a few months of having moved in. It was an indescribable smell that he had never encountered before, but he knew it emanated from inside the fridge.

The landlady had to call in an engineer to review the situation. He pronounced, amongst other things, that it was 'lethally damaged' – those not his exact words – and that we were 'lucky to still be here'. The refrigerant fluid had seeped into the interior and was now a health hazard.

That sent George more emboldened now to demand better accommodation as that room was now clearly uninhabitable. He wouldn't be disappointed as they reacted quickly to providing a much better flat over what had been a bank almost directly opposite the square, but shielded from it by mature trees.

Accessed from the ground floor by a door which opened up directly onto the street where a bus stop was sited, its double bedroom did not have a view except of the red brick building opposite and the back rooms with kitchen were small, with a single bedroom to the rear. It was quiet there, but at least was not overlooked by a number ten bus of a morning, forcing them to keep the curtains closed until they both were dressed. The jewel in this particular crown was the front sitting room, which was flooded with light and was the size of at least two, if not three double rooms.

Its windows were leaded, single glazed but that mattered not since the sun blessed this room all day, performing an arc as it did from left to right across the vast expanse of windows. The first investment had to be an enormous corner sofa which seated six easily, just to fill the room space with something. It was either that or hold five-a-side football tournaments at weekends to fill the void.

By now, it was clear that George's girlfriend had moved in for good, hoping to find work either at the school as a newly qualified teacher or some other employment.

Moose Conquering Fear

As it turned out, there were no openings as a teacher, so she found temporary work as a social care worker in the nearby county town, some ten or so miles away. This was by no means ideal, especially as it was said by her manager that social workers tended to last about eighteen months on average, before being burned out or feel the urge to move on. She lasted two years at it and surprisingly continued even after their marriage into the third year of George's stay at the school.

First Encounter of the Close Kind

Marriage was not extensively planned but had an air of inevitability about it. Together for nearly two years and knowing each other remotely for another year seemed to be a sound reason to think this relationship had legs, which was new for both of them. Arrangements were made which involved a trip to the north of the country again. Her family had that welcome common to the North of England, where opinions are open, direct and honest. He particularly got on well with Mel's brother and sister. His brother because it was like learning another language which George revelled in and the sister, because she was shortly off to university further south to follow her passion.

The only disruptor to the day was on leaving the small, modern church, when the vicar grabbed him by the arm suddenly as he approached the door. 'You can't go out there lad. It's tipping it down.'

'Like stair rods', said another voice. 'This was totally unexpected. Wasn't forecast this morning, was it', cried an astonished bystander who had wandered past the conversation inadvertently and decided to join in.

After five minutes or so, it came to an abrupt halt as if to make a point. The sky remained overcast till they came out of the reception. All George recalled of the day was the midnight blue going-away dress, as he had helped pick the colour. Seemed to have been his only real input into the day.

The next three to six months proved to be difficult.

Returning after six o'clock in the evening to an empty flat for two-three nights a week, sitting stretched out on the huge couch after making himself another mince chilli or spag bol wasn't how he had envisaged married life to be. Especially when Mel's shift pattern continued to cut across weekends with sleep overs expected on Saturday nights.

George knew there was nothing to be done. They needed the money, since the accommodation outside the school was chargeable, though at reduced rates to soften the blow. 'Still,' he thought, 'I would have expected some change to account for the fact we were now married. But not so, apparently.' His mind wandered to the fate of one of his cousins, whose forces marriage had started off on a single posting. Harsh to say the least on one level; completely counterintuitive and downright inhumane on another.

Weeks passed, the toleration began to lack, arguments started: small at first, but increasing in volume and dissatisfaction later.

It seemed as though they were simply existing.

Around the six month period, they had found time to sit down on the bed before turning in. Must have been a Sunday he recalled. She sat nearest the window on the other side of the bed. It was implicitly agreed he would sleep nearest the door to guard against any unwanted intruders, though the very thought of it filled him with unease. To be prepared for this kind of eventuality, he had willingly accepted the parting gift from his father of a rather long-bladed knife with a goat's foot handle.

'What's this then?' he remarked at the time, 'For luck, like a rabbit's foot?'

'No, be damned,' came a short reply, 'I've always kept it beside my bed in case anyone were to break in.' He then added thoughtfully, 'It's a skinning knife. You know, for skinning rabbits and the like.' George didn't feel the need to delve any deeper into its other possible uses.

She turned to look over her shoulder at him without turning her body towards him, as if she would recoil like a spring once the words were out. 'There's something I need to tell you.'

Never a good start, he thought. 'Something I've been meaning to tell you about. What, now that we're married and all.'

His mind was bouncing all over the place. He looked down at the carpet, up at the cracked varnish on the oak wardrobe and wondered why used things had to look so worn out. Nothing was perfect.

'What is it?' he said nervously. A pause echoed off the walls, which closed in on him.

'You know how I do night shifts at the children's home.'

'Well I've been sleeping in someone else's bed.'

'Yes, that must be weird.' were to be George's penultimate words that evening.

'I'm not alone in it though. His name is Max.' Another pause ensued before the void was filled. 'But nothing's happened since I've been married. I insisted I didn't think it was right to carry on as before.'

'So we just sleep together… for warmth as much as anything.'

'For how long?'

'These last three months since we've been married…' An empty silence left room for more. '… and for three months before that.'

The pit in his stomach grew larger and more profound. There was no more to say. No point in pushing for details to plague his sleeping hours. His imagination already had much to work with. That short, weak, spindly excuse for a man, no more than a boy but George was not much older than him and therefore no better.

He made his way to the back bedroom, taking pillow and a duvet with him from the top of the wardrobe.

The room was colder than the rest and mustier. He pushed at the rusted catch on the window to force it open and let in a little night air, before slumping down on the side of the bed.

What to do.

The buzzing inside his head increased. What he had believed in for years, attending church as a chorister evaporated, scattered round the room like ancient relics. His parents words came home to roost – 'we were sure you'd come home with a French or Canadian girl'. They and he was wrong. The ceremony, so far away that the majority of his family could not attend. Only the stalwarts bore witness to what was now an abomination. The words of the service ringing in his ears:

'if either of you… know of any just impediment… why you should not be joined in holy matrimony, you are to declare it… those whom God had joined, let no man put asunder.' Damn it!

This marriage was not even legal in God's eyes. He wrestled with his conscience, but then there's forgiveness. What? How? 'F**k that!' were the only two audible words to leave his mouth since he entered the room. More expletives followed aimed at her of course and at his own ineptitude for not spotting this earlier. The episode at college when he screamed out in French, her trip back north to see a girlfriend which ended up in a pub as a lock-in with the owner and his friend from the same school. Her girlfriend had sex in front of them on a bar couch and she said nothing happened. Who can watch that and not get aroused. 'F**k her!' emanated from his lips again. The rain, oh my God, the torrential rain trapping them in the church at the wedding service. The sun always shines on a marriage day for those few hours. He had attended so many as the paid choir member back in his home village. Never rained once at any time of year, damn it.

He was shaking but pulled himself up straight as he realised the impending anguish and immediate implications. Thoughts tumbled out in quick succession: Mum, how can I ever go back to her and explain this mess? Just a few months into our marriage 'Sorry everyone, made a big, big mistake. Best if we give the wedding presents back… those that aren't split between us after the divorce maybe?'

'Shit. What am I to do?' he tortured himself, turning his mind inside out, going over and over again in his head what he could possibly say.' Nothing.

Best to rest on it for now. Rest, what's that? He continued to torment himself – a cuckold for God's sake, for life. He'd read about them in literature so often and now, him, the shame of it all was overwhelming.

One thing was for sure – 'You can't stay here,' he railed at her, 'You'll have to go back to your mother, your parents. I can't have you in this flat. Go, for God's sake, go!'

The days and weeks passed. An odd phone call came in from the north. It was the holidays, so she'd have plenty to occupy herself with, plenty of friends she could catch up and hook up with. His thoughts circled around the deed and the timing. The call was very short as he insisted on having one question and only one question answered: 'Have you told your parents yet?'

'No, not yet', was the perpetual and customary reply he came to expect. 'Well, don't come back here until you do.'

Two months passed and no change, till she turned up at the door unannounced. 'What the hell are you doing here? Told your mother, father, brother, sister yet? No? Then f**k off!'

After the storm had passed, he capitulated to letting her stay a night before the return journey. But that never happened.

The ignominy was too great. His stupid pride got in the way and he chose the easier route in the hope that one day, he might come round to forgive her. But forget, no. That was engraved on his forehead and embedded in his skull.

He was a changed person.

Wanting to put all of those events behind him, George sought solace in finding another job, far away from that village, the neighbouring town and all its connotations. A change of scenery, he thought, would help ease the pain within. It was on this precept and with this burden to bear for the rest of his days that he went off to teach in Kenya with his unfaithful wife of but one year.

Change of Scenery

The sunshine helped. So did the people.

He arrived ahead of her, being dropped off in Nairobi to wait for a lift to the school up in the magnificent Rift Valley in the White Highlands. Even the name smacked of its colonial past, so George knew he would have to have his eyes wide open to the prospect that perhaps not all would necessarily welcome him there.

As he stepped out of the airport taxi on the corner of a bank and a hotel, he was immersed and surrounded by local Kenyans. 'This must be what it was like for those first few black immigrants coming into the foreign place that was Birmingham or Bradford or elsewhere,' he thought, reflecting on his early childhood when television came at last into his house. Only one channel was allowed, but he vaguely recalled the news items but remembered more the fixed opinions of the older members of his family who attempted to force them on anyone who would listen. George had not listened.

It was scary for sure, but his fears instantly subsided when he asked a gentleman in a dark but bleached suit, 'Do you have the time?' George hated wearing watches because they made his arm sweat. The only one he had been given as a teenage present was fixed to a wide band of leather with metal studs protruding around every inch of it on all sides. Hideous. He persisted with it thinking it would be seen as modern, but he was mistaken. He ditched in a drawer a few days later and it became conveniently lost.

'Sure thing, my friend. Quarter past three it is. You waiting on someone?' blazed an incredibly friendly smile behind an immaculate set of teeth. From that moment on, there was no stopping George. As his lift had not yet arrived, he ordered a coffee while he was waiting. 'Do you want it black like me, or white like you?' blurted out a waiter on his best form. A great sense of humour too, George concluded confidently, 'I'm going to love this place, I can tell.'

His energies could be poured into new and adventurous things as well as some more traditional pastimes. He continued to play hockey, though with some wild farmers who ran around barefoot across pitches bordered by eucalyptus and acacia trees. There was no getting away from thorns on the sidelines and George had a pair of Bata's best on to protect his feet from them. But these locals were something else. They would travel easily up to 250 miles on a weekend for a friendly match. They'd kick off by drinking half pints of Pimms from a clean bucket before running the opposition ragged on the hockey field. To be more precise, the field consisted of a volcanic-red murram surface with a type of couch grass or creeping grass extending in patches across it, but in no way providing an even surface. That was out of the question and made everything more fun.

The new things were twofold really: the people and the wonderfully rich fauna and flora against a backdrop of the infinite variety of nature and its remarkable ability to cope in such climes, from tropical shores of lake Victoria and the rocky shores of Lake Turkana to the alpine glacial valleys of Mount Kenya. All were adventures waiting to happen.

George had to learn fast to get settled in. Drew, the school secretary and seasoned professional in all things academic and cultural, was invaluable in this respect. He was glad to know that the school would loan him the 89,000 shillings to buy a second-hand car, but was amazed to hear that at the end of the two years, should he wish to leave, it could be sold for the same price, more than likely back to the school. With no frosts or salted roads to contend with, a vehicle there had every chance of enjoying a long, corrosion-free life.

He was less enamoured by her next statement about having servants at the house where he was being put up. He had always been brought up to do everything for himself, to cope with the big, wide world and yet here he was, having to employ a servant or servants. This went right against the grain for him, till he learnt why. 'If you don't employ at least one servant,' confided Drew, 'then you will be seen as depriving people of a job, where they can earn and send money back to their families.'

'Oh I see', said George more than a little reluctantly, promising himself in the same breath that he would treat this person or persons as if they were family.

As it turned out, it was only in his second year there that he lived outside the school and was responsible for hiring his own servant. He was recommended and graced with a marvellous young Kenyan called Joseph, whom the older white community would refer to as a houseboy, undertaking both culinary and domestic duties. George emphasised only three things before he got started. One, he need not worry himself with the garden as George enjoyed that. Two, that he could return to his family at any time and for any duration as necessary and be paid for that time away. Third, he will always be Joseph to them and he should use their first names. Joseph accepted the first two but struggled with the last and often called them *bwana* and *meme-sab* which seemed like a lifelong habit, perhaps a tradition too ingrained for him to break with.

Although disagreeing with the principle, George saw the reason for it and came to accept it as his way of providing for his family remotely. One advantage he appreciated more and more was the ability to invite friends or even recent acquaintances to stay for a meal or stay the night, giving sufficient notice naturally. Joseph rose to it all on every occasion very willingly and most competently. They became firm friends and were sorry to leave each other when their two years were up.

That is not to say that their stay could not have been extended. They had enjoyed the holidays going on safari with colleagues in the first year and alone together in the second year. There was much to see, absorb and reflect on in such a beautiful country. That would be the subject for another day. For now, he was tempted to stay on, but there were other considerations to take on board related to his career and his wife's desire to be nearer her family which tipped the balance. There had also been two experiences he would not wish on anyone, which dampened their enjoyment and left them physically and, to a certain degree, mentally scarred.

The first began as they set off in the Suzuki jeep as they had done many times before. They had got used to the dust levels penetrating the vehicle through the rear door as if it had been wide open for the entire journey. It didn't matter as all cars had the same issue.

'Dust gets everywhere;' Drew had remarked nonchalantly, unabashed as the enthusiastic instigator of his car purchase from day one, 'can't do much about it.' A woman of few words, she was not wrong. No matter. Things were covered up enough, essentials packed such as Gerry can, tent, mozzie nets, panga and lots of bottled water. Most of these items had been bought at a garage sale, a common enough event when anyone decided to up sticks and leave the country. The panga served a dual purpose: yes, cutting down intransigent bush in your way looked like its most likely use, but more importantly it allowed the carrier to dig a hole in the ground where a toilet could be performed without leaving evidence of the same.

The crate of bottled water looked less appealing. George never got used to the state of the glass bottles, whose reuse far exceeded the number of times London tap water was purported to have been drunk. Not ten times recycled, not even ten times ten times. More like tens of thousands of times with the upper third of the glass bottle so striated with industrial washing and rinsing, that it was almost impossible to see what was inside it. This had not however been a cause of concern until the day that George had to pull the car up short, as he himself was caught short.

Returning to the car to continue the journey was interrupted just a minute later with another abrupt halt, a descent, the requisite gardening and cover up. Once it had started, there was no end to the interruptions. They seemed to be brought on by excessive heat or direct sunlight, both insanely unavoidable in this best of all possible worlds, where the sun rises each morning just before 7am and sets at the same time in the evening. The intervening hours filled with endless sunshine and largely cloud-free skies, the only exception being during the rainy season, when you could set your watch to 4pm when the rain-laden dark skies released their load onto a thirsty land.

This unwelcome situation persisted for two whole months, until an evening meal with a friend who regularly hosted tourists explained that, from the symptoms described, George had more than likely contracted amoebic dysentery.

'Usually by drinking contaminated water', he explained. The vision of the water bottles returned before his eyes and he cursed out loud. 'No problem,' he went on,' I've got just the job for you. Here, I give one of these tablets to all my tourists on their first day to prevent them catching it and ruining their holiday.'

'Oh, thank you so much', George grimaced gratefully as he tried to suppress another bout and failed. Downing the tablet, he continued to chat and things began to subside without him noticing. His friend even went as far as to describe what he would go through next. 'A distinctive green discharge will announce the end of the infection and you should slowly return to something resembling normal.'

He was not wrong either. The end of their afternoon saw them pull up no more than a hundred metres down his friend's drive when he was forced to pull over again. Sure enough everything just as described happened to George and immensely relieved, he climbed back up into the driver's seat, breathing a sigh of relief, 'Thank God that's over with.'

The second experience which predated the dysentery occurrence, took place during the April or May of their second year. It had been more than a year since the debacle of their marriage. Relations between George and Mel had eased, the more time that was spent together, helped by the most pleasant of settings imaginable: sitting under the subtle shade of a pepper tree on a patio, sipping G&Ts or pure lime juice of an evening.

She had dropped into the conversation that she might be pregnant but warned that we should tell no one for three months to be sure. One Saturday night after guests had made their way home, she retired to her bed while George continued to stay up and read.

The padding of heavy feet along the wooden floors between their bedrooms made him look up from his book. 'Are you ok?'

No answer was forthcoming, so he rose to his feet and made his way to the bathroom, whose light pierced the darkness. Looking round the door, he caught her looking down at the pan, which led his eyes to the same discoloured water. 'My God. Are you bleeding?' Then the panic set in. 'Shall I call a doctor or drive you to the hospital?' These suggestions they both knew were hopeless as it was a Saturday. There was no local doctor other than the matron at the school and driving to Nairobi would take more than an hour and a half.

'No. I think we'll have to deal with this ourselves', came the calm but frightened reply. That night would live with them forever. George did not know what time it all concluded. The sun came up barely an hour or so later. Mel had taken a bath – thankfully in water that was not totally brown as it tended to be most days – and was now sleeping. George was stunned on many fronts over the next few days and weeks, doing his utmost to console Mel, taking her to the hospital on the Monday where they confirmed a miscarriage had occurred.

It was amazing that it took such an event for all those nearest to them at school to relate similar stories. 'I had no idea', he said, 'that so many experience it.' It didn't help the loss felt but it felt like a burden shared and the consultant surgeon's words soothed the pain. 'No reason why you shouldn't go on to have a healthy child next time… when you're good and ready of course. Not before.'

George could not help thinking that this was meant to be.

Return to Abnormality

On their return to the UK, a troubled calm descended on them like an uneasy peace. Day to day life consumed almost every waking hour. Money was tight. A return to social care was out of the question and the odd tuition lesson at the school provided little relief from their predicament: how to afford a first house in one of the most expensive counties in England?

They sat one night in the roomy but cold downstairs flat that had been allocated to them, a flat with an unkempt and unloved garden, for which George had no enthusiasm or inclination to put any effort into its restoration. There were bigger fish to fry. How to save enough for a deposit? Neither parents were in any position to help out, so they did not ask.

A knock came at the door. It was the insurance man, whose appointment George had absentmindedly forgotten. Totally unprepared, he invited the man in. A different one to last time. It always seemed to be that way. 'How did they manage to survive with such a staff attrition rate', he wondered. He had remained loyal to them since his parents had first taken out a life policy in his name – one they could hardly afford – at the tender age of seven or eight. When he came of age, it became fully paid up. 'It wasn't much, certainly not enough to get them out of the current situation, but was enough at a pinch…' he thought,' … to take care of his funeral costs in the long term.' Any provision for Mel was out of the question, financially and ethically in his mind.

The man was indistinctly featured: below average height, balding a little and sat in a tight-fitting, old suit. Curiously unprepossessing as he was, George could not help admire the way that these men – he had never come across a lady representative to date – were always so obligingly helpful, without the hard sell, that he felt immediately at ease with him. They were good listeners.

It was also a mark of their company that they insisted on home visits in the evening. Even much later, when the digital age swept all companies before it into an unknown and unforgiving maelstrom of never-ending bureaucracy, which insists on seeking out an alternative provider of any service as a routine annual chore.

He liked this personal side to the company. As George had been visited by these fellows on and off through these early employment years, there was a feeling of being part of another, different family. Another plus on their account.

Moose Conquering Fear

As the man listened, so George relaxed enough to pour out the troubles they were in at that time, which was the reason that any additional investment or policies were a pipe dream away.

'Well,' the visitor's tone was upbeat and encouraging, 'there's always room for more chaps like you. You could come to work for us. Not to replace your current occupation naturally, but as a second evening job.' he added considerately.

'Have a think about it. Don't decide right now. Talk it through and if you want to take me up on the offer, you have my number. We can organise a day's training back at HQ and you can be up and running the day after.'

The offer struck a chord with George. He was still young and had the energy to do another job. There wasn't much to come home to. No committed conversations were being had, so he knew he would not be missed. Mel agreed with the proposal without having to think too long. 'It's a necessity as far as I'm concerned if we're ever to get out of this rut.' George didn't reply or prolong that topic exploration, for fear that they would be talking about different ruts.

It was settled. Off he packed to Croydon one early September Saturday. The sky was pleasantly bright on the journey there, with a few clouds gathering in the afternoon to darken the utilitarian classroom he had been shown into for the second time that day. He had taken copious notes, felt semi-prepared but his mind was racing anxiously. He seriously wondered if he would have the nerve to knock on people's doors of an evening, when they might be sitting down to tea or have come back late from work dog-tired or had some disaster at their progeny's school which demanded their immediate attention, rather than open their door to a complete stranger and take him into their confidence.

Nothing seemed more likely that he would not make a single policy sale. 'Time to dig deep and find that extrovert', he surmised to himself on the way back. He found himself looking at the houses at the side of the road, imagining himself on the threshold and rehearsing the lines which would hopefully open a helpful and productive conversation. The benefits it must be said had been slightly over-egged by the representative the week before. 'After the first few policies are underway – so long as they're happy and you maintain contact with them to do that – the premiums continue to be paid by them, on which you earn commission every month. It's not hard to see that after only a few months or years in this job,' the tight suit said persuasively,' you can earn £1000 a month without getting out of bed!'

'Not enough to fork out for a new suit, clearly,' George smiled to himself.

'But remember, the golden rule of sales,' he stressed, 'that every NO is one step away from a YES.' He took that piece of positive thinking to heart and indeed, it never left him as he progressed his career subsequently in a different direction.

Daylight was still plentiful when George made his first foray into an estate which he'd identified as a good place to start. As he made his way up the first short pathway to a bungalow, his heart was pounding and the butterflies kicked in. 'What if …' echoed inside his head. He tried to banish it semi-successfully. A knock on the frosted glass brought a large male figure into focus and the door was thrown open by a loud voice. 'Yes? What is it? What do you want?'

'I've come to ask if you have any life insurance currently or are looking to..' His words were cut short by the curt reply, 'No and we don't need any,' after which the door was closed firmly in his face.

'Guess that's a NO.' mumbled George to himself. 'Now I know what to expect, the next time will not be so bad hopefully', said his slightly deflated but recovering ego.

A similar bungalow with a red door seemed inviting. Looks can be deceptive. Another NO. Followed by a green and a blue door… he began to calculate theories in his mind. 'It seems as if door colour is not a strong indicator of willingness to spend on life insurance.'

The evening wore on. He continued in vain to be invited in, before coming to a pleasant-looking extension with a bay window at the front. A car was parked in the drive, so he mustered his most confident but warm knock on its polished wooden door. The kindly looking face of a gentleman in his late fifties greeted him and he remarked how he and his wife had only been discussing the same the weekend before.

'What a piece of luck.' George contemplated as another, more plausible theory entered his head. 'At least I've got past the door.'

When asked to, he sat himself down on their ample, mock leather sofa next to the gent with his wife opposite, who had made them all tea. The conversation continued in a forthright manner, holding nothing back and adding his own experience of the company over twenty years or more. 'I see. Poacher turned gamekeeper, eh…? Or maybe it's the other way round. Anyway, you know what

I mean.' George did. He made to get up from the sofa but sat back down as he'd forgotten his last sentence he'd rehearsed, thinking that realistically it would have no effect. He thought twice about it.

'So, would you like to take out any insurance with "us"?' The words seemed at once strange but helpful and he hoped, not too gauche. Had he become part of the family too now? He dared not look up, waiting for the inevitable.

'Yes, I very much think we should like to do that. What details do you need?'

George could not believe his ears and reconfirmed in what must have come across as utter astonishment, 'So you'd like to take out insurance today? Tonight.' he faltered on the time as it had passed by so quickly, gazing out the bay window and seeing the evening had drawn in already.

As he gave a cheery wave goodbye from their front path with the signed documents under his arm, he turned back to his car. 'Best to end on a good note… and it is getting late now,' he thought out aloud and with a spring in his tired step, glancing at his watch. 'Nearly nine. Time to head back.'

He didn't bother Mel with the details, just the success. He continued for two months each evening spending two to three hours going door to door. However, as the nights began to lengthen and the number of estates dwindled in his village, he reluctantly came to the conclusion that travelling further afield to expand his territory would inevitably cut down on his doorstepping time. To be frank with himself, he had not sold many more policies in the meantime and let the rep know that he would be stopping. Hard to admit failure at the time with little support for evening work at the house, he sought other means, including increasing Mel's work to make ends meet and save for a deposit.

Either way, this life to him seemed abnormal and he could see no end to it.

Out of the Blue

The surgeon in Nairobi was right. The timing may not have been perfect by any stretch of the imagination, but within two years a baby was on the way, which increased the need to find a house to permanently live in. Those were still out of reach until a scheme was introduced to take part ownership in a property, with the school funding the lesser part.

Needless to say, the search, acquisition and move kept the two of them occupied as well as preparing for the new arrival. Perhaps this was the change that George was looking for to repair the past. Only time would tell.

In line with many other parents' views, a second child came less than two years after the first to keep each other company. Trips out were involved, with their family saloon barely living up to its name without obscuring the views of the driver. Only George's packing skills, learnt from the electronics distribution job, made the trips legally viable.

Over the next three years, in spite of the new arrivals who were much loved and cherished, external trips were a source of silent embarrassment. Any gatherings heaped live coals on George's head as the trite, light conversations avoided all possible shame that would inevitably lead to calumny, humiliation and disapproval if the matter ever surfaced. To boot, Mel's parents and family were blissfully unaware, *still*, of what had transpired before and immediately after the sham marriage.

His reluctance to disappoint his parents – and especially his mother – drove his silence on the matter, but it was burning him up inside. The overwhelming feeling he had was that she had him over a barrel. The ignominy of such an admission would be on his head, the injured party as he saw it and she was getting away with it.

Her demeanour had clearly brushed it well under a carpet, ignored the transgression and moved on. For him, the words from the service continued to haunt him,

> If you know of any just cause or impediment why you should not be married, then you are to declare it or forever hold your peace.

He was of the opinion that their marriage was not lawful in the sight of God, but they were bound together in a continual purgatory.

Sometimes events tip the balance. One such happened on 16 October 1989, just a year after the birth of their second child, a daughter. Not a natural disaster, but a seismic change in the life of any young lad: the call from his father saying his mother had died in her sleep the night before.

Taken from him too soon at what he considered to be a desperately young age of just sixty-one years old, he mourned his loss privately. It was a mixture of grief and relief. Her health had always been fragile, under too much medication from misguided professionals. Her reprieve came too late – removing those pills which cancelled each other out – but was with heartfelt thanks to the infinitely better care given her by St. Bart's in London. His father's account of her passing was both touching and disarming. 'She went up to bed in the back bedroom with her evening coffee. The next morning, she lay there, still, as if she'd not moved in the night… just a spot of coffee on the pillow beside her. She was gone.'

'Sounds very peaceful.' George squeezed out with some difficulty, fighting back the moisture in the corner of both eyes. His Dad's voice cracked 'Yeah. It was.'

Turning to practical matters as was his wont, he began, 'Have to contact the family…'

'Leave that to us. I can come up tomorrow to discuss the arrangements.'

An unusually worried tone in his voice thought aloud, 'Crikey… I don't even know if she wanted to be buried or cremated.'

'Cremated Dad, she wanted to be cremated.'

'Are you sure, son?'

'Yes Dad. She told me so.'

Of course they had never discussed such things and this came unexpectedly out of the blue. 'I'll handle all the funeral and legal arrangements', George found himself reassuring his father on a subject he had no experience of whatsoever. He just felt it was his duty to do it for Mum. No question of it.

'Ok. I'll see you tomorrow as early as I can.' They kept it mutually brief for the same reason.

For George and his sister the coming weeks were dominated by concerns they had about their father's ability to cope without Mum there. 'The main thing I think is that we know he can feed himself.'

'Yes, 'cos Mum did all the cooking. I don't think he even knows what a pan is!' she joked with him.

Organising probate for the first of a couple to pass away was fairly straightforward as it turned out. The main concern being that no account is frozen, leaving the partner without access to funds.

Frequent visits to the family home and village were made by both of them to talk about their mum, share cherished memories, look through photos and smooth over the transition to a single life.

'It was horrible.' their father shared with them a day or two later after the funeral. 'The police came that morning and asked me all these questions and I thought "Hang on a minute. You think I had something to do with her death!"'

They repeated what they had been told, that this is normal when a person dies at home. They have to establish no foul play is involved. 'I'll try to arrange to die in a hospital when my time comes,' George planned in all seriousness, 'to avoid that pain for those left behind.'

Within three or so weeks, George recounted his last visit to the home to his sister.

'I saw Cedric the other day.' his father began, 'He lost Mavis only last year. "Come round for lunch" he'd suggested, so I did, to help us both… as I thought. Well, when he came out with lunch I couldn't believe my eyes. "Strike a light! Is that all you're having?" I said.'

'Yes,' answered Cedric not batting an eyelid, 'that's what I always have, every day. A lettuce leaf and slice of ham.'

'Well, I came back and thought I'm not ending up like that!' he said emphatically, 'So I got the slow cooker out, put some beef skirt in there with some veg from the garden and ate my fill that same evening.'

He could see the surprised look on George's slightly disbelieving face, adding, 'You see, you don't realise it at the time but you take in a lot more than you think.

Moose Conquering Fear

I could see your mum standing there at the stove and preparing the food, long enough to remember what she did. What I couldn't remember, a recipe book filled in the blanks for me.'

'You're right Dad,' he agreed, 'I had the same experience when I first came to iron my own shirts at college. Sitting there as a kid on one of the armchairs after coming in from school, there she was, often as not, doing the ironing. It's amazing what the brain takes in without us knowing.'

This news was music to his sister's ears as they both now could relax in the knowledge that he could look after himself. 'He'll be okay. Don't worry.'

'Yes, you're right, he will'.

New Outlook

Things were never the same. With his dad settled, George felt that he could confront his uncomfortable situation more directly.

With the new academic year upon him, he could reflect on his work which had branched out considerably into what was fast becoming known as the IT domain. It had begun on his return from abroad where he had led Maths and kitted out a new IT department, developing new admission entry tests for one and a new syllabus for the other.

Having been given the empty space next to the front hall lobby, which was a major crossroads in good weather and even more so in inclement weather, he set about connecting wires across desks pushed up against the outer walls, trailing them around the edge of the five metre square room. The four BBC microcomputers (models A and B) were served by two simple 8" floppy disks for system and storage.

Spotting the increasing popularity with students, the Head had the courage to suggest converting the old, prefabricated, dual Science labs into a permanent IT space and invited George to manage the project to his own specification and design. 'It will be a stopping point on the parents' tour and can showcase technology.' he suggested.

With ample budget, George was able to take on the challenge. He used the latest network server from a company in Cambridge housed in his own office next to where the two labs had been knocked through to make one long room. He made this into a pleasant working environment, leaving a large space in the middle to promote interaction and to cater for robotic turtle activities. The BBC Micros were transferred and stationed all around the outside, shielded from the sun's rays by office-type vertical blinds.

He was up and running in no time, creating introductions to BASIC programming and word processing. He went on to design a project that involved the whole school – including the Secretary and some senior school staff – to reintroduce the branch railway line to the village which had been axed during the Beeching campaign. It seemed to grab everyone's attention, even though a section approaching the county town had had a house extension built over it, which effectively scuppered the plan… on the face of it.

But with that project drawing to a close, George found himself wondering 'What next?' As luck would have it, a colleague of his who had recently joined the teaching staff shared his view and optimism for the future.

'This will shake things up a bit.' was the Head's wife's summary on the new appointment. Given she was the sole female representative on the staff, this was understandable. There was no shortage of attention of course paid to the new arrival. A handshake in his classroom by way of introduction began what was to become a beautiful friendship between them. There was an unspoken understanding of each other's situation and mutual assistance, when needed, in areas which seemed unsympathetic in a male-dominated environment.

As the days shortened towards an onset of winter, George invited G, as she liked to be known, to share duties at the badminton club he had initiated. She was an accomplished tennis player and, though many would say those sports don't mix, neither of them had any difficulty with the transition.

The boys benefited enormously from the extra hands on deck and the two enjoyed their after-school evenings more, sometimes individually to cover for each other and at other times jointly sharing the load.

As the nights drew in, there was one badly lit section of pathway approaching the tiny back door, which lay hidden in the corner of a small yard. The yard was often muddy as it was a stop-off point for the boys for removing rugby boots, knocking the worst off the soles before entering the boot room via another door to the side.

As they drew near to the pitch black of the corner – where a raised coconut mat presented an unwelcome obstacle to many a parent unfamiliar with the terrain – he reached out a guiding hand as G hesitated to step forward. She placed her hand trustingly in his and a warmth passed between them.

They closed out the evening before heading back to their respective accommodation. As they both drove back in different cars, George followed G down the steep drive by the apple orchard and turned left through the village. At the other end of the village lay a mini-roundabout where their ways parted, hers to the left and his to the right. As he drew up alongside in the outer lane, he glanced to his left at the same moment G glanced to her right and they both waved good night at the same time. Neither car stopped, but continued on their respective short journeys home.

New Outlook

George relayed in passing to his wife how the evening had gone and what a good friend G had become. Her reply was as unexpected as it was inappropriate.

'Better watch out with that one. She's young and impressionable. I'd see less of her if I were you!' came the veiled threat from a reproachful and ill-considered mouth.

'You what?' George's sinews on the back of his neck stiffened. 'You have got to be joking. She's a friend for God's sake. What is the matter with you?' The tirade became a torrent in short order. 'So it's ok for you to sleep with someone three months before your marriage and six months after, but I can't choose my friends, what… in case the same thing happens?'

A full-blown argument could have ensued, but George stormed off into the back bathroom, closing the door behind him to calm down. Sitting uncomfortably on the toilet seat, he rose to his feet, cursing, before pacing about the small room. He was beside himself with the consternation and reminiscent indignity of it all. His worst fear was being realised. He blamed himself for not being stronger earlier on and persisting with what seemed like a French farce, but with all the comedy removed. All that was left was the anguish of an impossible situation.

And then there were the children. What a disappointment he would become to them, even though he would see them, inevitably it would be less. He didn't want that but saw no way round it. Things couldn't go on in the same way, not even for the sake of the children. Living a lie for the next 15 years was unthinkable.

From that evening family life, such as it was, ground to a halt. Things had reached a new low, from which they could not recover. Her parting words one morning were 'I thought you'd harden.'

'Yes… and not be the soft pushover you thought I had become. You're damn right about that.' He left the house without another word.

Over the following weeks and months their relations deteriorated and, as if in counterbalance, his friendship with G increased. They saw more of each other: many would have questioned George's motivation no doubt, but they simply enjoyed each other's company to begin with. A light had been lit at the end of a very long tunnel.

Parting

When the divorce came, it was not swift.

He had moved out, staying initially with G, until the school provided a temporary cottage on the same green opposite a cricket square. Feelings at the school were awkward but remained professional. They were mildly sympathetic, perhaps as a result of a young male intern who had decided to intervene on Mel's behalf one evening and got the whole story, both barrels, before being sent packing.

His second brush with justice was not in the least bit gratifying. Deterred by advice not to go back into the past, he was forced to assume the role of defendant. Even less impressive was the counsel who turned up late. A man with slick hair who reminded him of his father's reference to the 'Brylcreem Boys'; a man who rushed in to the briefing room with clearly no idea of the background, had only read the summary and was worse placed to present a case before a female judge in her chambers.

A large lady at the head of a table with a scowl for a face glanced summarily in George's direction. 'This doesn't bode well.' he thought, 'There's only one way this will go.' He was not wrong. As the lies poured forth, he could only look up to the ceiling which was taken to be dismissive male arrogance. His counsel – not George who clearly did not merit talking to by the judge – was warned that his client would be threatened with contempt of court if that happened again.

It was all downhill from then. He was held to paying the mortgage – which he had offered to do before the proceedings – and slapped no doubt justifiably in the judge's unbiased view with two heavy maintenance payments monthly, until the children reached eighteen years of age. He had no argument with those. 'At least I'll still get to see the children…' he consoled himself as joint custody was awarded on the same day.

The impoverished state this left George in now only served to make him more determined to better his lot, either through promotion to another school or by changing careers and going into business. In these aims he was wholly supported by the now long-suffering G, who seemed to have thrown her lot in with his.

Months elapsed until the legal process' first step to finality was pronounced at decree nisi. George recalled the day. He was at work in the airy computer room,

Parting

when the phone in his office rang. The blinds were open as the sun had not moved round to that side as yet. He answered in the usual business-polite way. The voice on the other end jarred in his ear and he was immediately shaken to his core. The tone was curt.

'It's me. Now the nisi has come through, I'd just like to tell you that's the last time you will see or speak to your children again. Like a last word with them? I'll put them on.'

His breath was taken from him. He was stunned beyond words, but had to compose himself quickly as he heard their mother call out to them to come to the phone. There was precious little time, so little time left, so little.

He was back in the blue Escort, stopped in a lay-by, with both of the children in the back seats, his daughter sitting uncomfortably on a badly fitting polystyrene child booster seat. The words of his son, when first he broke the news about his parents parting, returned to him as they had done every day since. 'I'll wiss you.'

'This is unbearable.' he winced at the prospect, 'So much for joint custody!'

He had just a few moments before his son and then his daughter came on the phone. He repeated the same words to each as he knew it would be all too brief. 'Hello darling. I'm sorry to say this may be the last time I am allowed to speak to you. Please remember that I love you and always will. Look after your little/ big sister/brother. Bye my darling.' It was not long after that the phone was snatched out of their grasp.

George continued to hold the phone to his ear, listening to the silence at the other end when the call ended in stupefied disbelief. Suddenly there were noises and a voice in the background in his earpiece. His whole body froze; quietly he leant more over his desk to strain his ears.

She's taken the phone off the hook', he whispered to himself. 'What a stroke of luck.' 'Come on,' he pleaded, 'come back to the phone my darlings. Be curious as to why the phone will now be dangling down resting on the arm of the sofa.' He carried on as if in conversation with them, but without speaking, 'I know you're smarter than she gives you credit for. Come to the phone my darlings.' He could hear that their mother was in the kitchen, no doubt preparing food. 'Who would be first to come to the phone?' he wondered. He didn't have to wait long. No more than a minute before the soft, gentle youngest voice asked 'Hello?' 'Oh my, how clever you are... ' George continued for a little while longer and spoke to both before signing off, 'You'd better go. Leave the phone back down on the sofa where you found it. Take care, my darling.' And with that they bustled off into the background. That would be the last time they spoke.

'How can this be just?' he spattered out many times till the salty taste reached his mouth. Wiping his eyes with the back of his hand, he thought to rail at his legal advice. His solicitor advised him that he could challenge and fight for the joint custody judgment to be upheld, but that would cost thousands more to achieve. He had no funds left to mount a challenge, replacing the receiver gently onto its cradle. He realised there was nothing more he could do, so helpless had the situation become. She had won hands down.

All that was left was to suppress all his natural paternal instincts and deal with his new circumstance in a brutally harsh reality. No matter how hard, he had to face it, that he may never see his children again. No matter how long for, he had to face it, that he would never hold them again. Their mother would have wished that he was dead to them. She found a replacement within two weeks, Tom, whom George did not know, but who would clearly become the replacement father figure she craved and they no doubt deserved as the young, innocent victims in all of this. But as the days and weeks came and went, more realisations hit him: his children's view of him will be stained, polluted beyond any resemblance to the truth; they would be brought up completely differently than he had envisaged for them and their characters would reflect their upbringing; if he met them years and years later, he was sure he would not recognise them nor they him, not just physically but psychologically.

The more he thought about it, the closer the conclusion drew near that he needed to forget they existed, beyond the two baby photographs he had on him. He would have to remember them like that, knowing nothing, no nothing, would ever be the same with them again. It took six years for this pain to even start to diminish and it lingered on in unexpected pockets of time, when he least expected them to surface again. His life had changed irrevocably.

New Beginnings

So much had changed. Some for the good, but one thing was certain. His distrust of the whole marriage ceremony and institution was severely dented. He had found a gem in G, but his view of the fairer sex was tainted, to say the least.

He immersed himself in finding new work, which was hard to focus on but necessary for him to extract himself from the location, from the disapproval of once close friends and from the workplace which was a constant reminder of the recent past. He had to get out of there. G was supportive, very much so, but this he had to do for himself as no plans could be made until he had taken that first step.

For advancement in education he aimed at deputy headships, which were slow to come round, like most senior level teaching posts. The other prong to his attack was entirely new and proved a tougher nut to crack. As no business applications had a hope of success, he sought the advice of an economically viable management consultant for two to three sessions on how to position yourself to make this career change. George got the impression on their first meeting, that it was the consultant's first stab at achieving this too. That was of itself a comforting thought: they were both in it together and would both gain from its successful conclusion.

They met in the consultant's house where mock interviews were captured on video and replayed to hone his skills. He had made short postcard-sized notes on how to prepare and get in the right frame of mind, which consisted of things such as:

> I have transferrable skills
>
> I have the skills to make a success of this position
>
> I know I can add value to this role

Armed with these pointers he tried to apply for a number of what seemed distinct possibilities, but was unsuccessful.

At his final session, business contacts were mentioned of which George had none. 'But surely you have some', he said confidently without making it a question, turning the tables on the recommender.

'Well yes, of course. There are a couple of my old colleagues, Ron and Melvyn I could reach out to. Give me a day or two and I'll come back to you.'

Within four days, George found himself sat in front of Melvyn, who reported directly to the Director Ron, putting his case for running their two types of network and making better use of them. This sounded like his home turf and he headed back home satisfied that he'd given a good account of himself and liked Melvyn too.

Two days later a curious thing happened, which, to this day, George believes was a sign for him to make up his mind, one way or the other for good.

He received two phone calls on a Thursday morning. One, an offer of a Deputy Headship at a substantially higher salary than he was on at the time. The other, an offer to join Melvyn but on £8,000 less than his current salary. 'It's make your mind up time', he shared with G on his next call, 'Education or Business.'

They both knew there was only one route which, in the longer term, would allow him to extend his skills and further his career. 'I feel I've so much more to do', he confided to G as they had discussed on many occasions before.

For G it meant staying in post till a new position presented itself nearer to George's new work, while for George, he was off to the big city: London.

About the Author

Peter Massam is a writer who captures a moment in time, a location, events or human interactions that have shaped his life and experiences that have been instrumental in managing the journey.

His previous publications are as a poet and technical author. More recently, the Cuz Collection brought together poetry and complementary sketches and images.

The first collection of short sketch poems captures the motivations behind the urge to draw a scene or capture a moment on camera, which sparks observations or symbolises a trend in attitudes or simply celebrates a moment of beauty or an historical event.

The second collection reflects on the plant choices made in a country garden over eleven years and the memories they evoke from child to adulthood.

A technical book began this journey to help two opposite sides value each other's domain for the good of the Customer, highlighting the importance of what was to become a permanent agenda item at board level – Customer Experience.

Learning Experience Trilogy
Nipper (2022)
ISBN-13: 978-1-9822-8609-5

First Cuz Collection of Poems
Sketch Poems (2019; Audible 2020)
ISBN-13: 978-1701299238

Second Cuz Collection of Poems
Reflections in a Country Garden (2021)
ISBN-13: 979-8723096103

Customer Experience
Managing Service Level Quality across Wireless and Fixed Networks (2007)
ISBN-13: 978-0470848487

Lightning Source UK Ltd.
Milton Keynes UK
UKHW011821210822
407563UK00002B/56